The Royal Diaries

MARY, QUEEN OF SCOTS

QUEEN WITHOUT A COUNTRY

BY KATHRYN LASKY

Scholastic Inc. New York

FRANCE
1553

I am for some reason thinking of numbers today as I write on this first page of the diary my dear mother sent me for my birthday, which was yesterday. So I am now eleven years and one day. I was a Princess for only ten months and one day. But I have been a Queen for ten years, three months, and one day. I was crowned Queen when I was a baby, before I could walk. Although I am told I could pull myself up by any table leg, chair, or the fringe of any wall tapestry in the castle. I am Mary, Queen of Scots, but I am far from Scotland. I live in France.

It could have worked out much differently, especially this being my eleventh birthday. For at one time I was to be given in marriage in an agreement called the Treaties of Greenwich to Edward VI, the English King. But the treaty was broken — all for the best, seeing as Edward died just six months ago at the age of sixteen. Now I am to marry Francis, the son of King Henry II of France and his Queen, Catherine de Medici. That was decided after the broken treaty with England, and that is why I live here now and have since I was five years old. This way I can be schooled in the ways of the French court. And thus Francis and I might become good friends before we become man and wife. We are good friends, best friends, and we need not worry about marriage for a long time — until I am at least thirteen or so.

I must go now, for my uncles de Guises are arriving for luncheon. They are one day late for my birthday, as the roads between here and Meudon were impassable because of heavy rains. My old nurse, Janet Sinclair, will have fits if my hair is not tended to properly. I have red hair — like pale fire, almost blonde. Some think it is my best feature. I think it is just hair and requires too much time even if I am a Queen.

P.S. How, thinking so much of numbers this day, could I forget to mention that my lucky number is four? Why is four my lucky number? Because of my four Marys, my best friends and companions since I was a baby. They came with me here to France all the way from Scotland. They are Mary Seton, Mary Fleming, Mary Beaton, and Mary Livingston. They are known by everyone as the Queen's Marys. I think of them as my lucky clover leaf.

My uncles de Guises — Francis, the warrior, and his wife, my dear aunt, Anne d'Este, who is expecting a child come spring, and Charles, Cardinal of Lorraine — were all waiting. It is lucky that I took care with my hair, or rather that my chambermaid, Minette, did. For indeed my grandmother, my mother's mother, Antoinette de Bourbon, had sent a diamond circlet as a gift to weave through my braids, which Minette had arranged in a ring on top of my head. "*Charmante!*" my uncles and aunt exclaimed as I entered the salon, and I felt my face flush red. This sudden flushing is a terrible burden for one of my complexion. It does not look like the rouge of the court ladies. Instead one might think I am catching on fire. And there is simply no controlling it. Oh, well. My aunt brought me yards of cloth of gold, for she says I am growing so fast and will need some new gowns for grand balls. Janet Sinclair, my nurse, sighed with delight at the thought of me floating about in cloth of gold, but I saw Madame de Parois's mouth twist into a hideous little smirk. Madame de Parois is my governess and she is a vexation. No, worse than a vexation. She is nasty. A small-minded woman with a face like rising dough — floury white and puffy. She resents any pleasure anyone has and always seems to think they are having these pleasures at her expense. One would have thought she had paid for the cloth of gold and not my uncles.

I almost know what each of my uncles is going to say before he says it. Uncle Francis — they call him le Balafré, the Scarred One, because of a wound he received at the Siege of Boulogne in 1545 — always asks whether my mother, Marie de Guise, has written and whether he can see her letters. Mother does not like me to show her letters to anyone. There are things that only mothers and daughters should discuss. But Uncle Francis always presses. So we have thought of a way around this. Mother sends me false letters to show him. It is quite devious. I do not like to think of myself playing tricks on my uncle, but I am so far from my mother, deprived for so many years of her company, that I feel there should be something that is just ours.

My uncle the Cardinal always inquires about my studies — especially my progress in Latin. They all love me terribly much. They praise me constantly. Even Uncle Francis with that scar that slashes across his face like a piece of lightning torn from the sky — his eyes soften when I come into the salon. I am so loved by my uncles and aunt and by the other children of Queen Catherine and King Henry — the Princesses Claude and Elizabeth and the Dauphin Francis and the babies. So why do I still feel homesick for Scotland? And why do I still feel the sharp pain of my mother's leaving from her visit as if it were yesterday and not two years ago?

P.S. I nearly forgot to mention that Aunt Anne, in addition to bringing me the cloth of gold, also brought me something else of gold — a little golden lapdog. Now between the four Marys and myself we have six lapdogs! This new one is so tiny she could fit in my muff! She is adorable. I think I shall call her Puff, for she reminds me of a fluffy little cloud.

DECEMBER 11, 1553
ROOFTOP OF THE CHÂTEAU

My uncles are still here. We had a little dance last night. My best dance partner of the evening was Aunt Anne. We know each other's rhythms. Francis is a terrible dancer. No rhythm and he has not the wind to jump in the galliards, which have much jumping. Always after a galliard or a pavane, he must take a rest. The King and Queen are not here at the moment but at Château Fontainebleau. That is why it was a *petit bal*, or little dance, instead of a grand one. It was all very merry, and the pastry chef made me a second birthday cake with sugar thistles and harebells, the flowers of Scotland. I wondered as I bit into the cake if I might ever see those flowers again. The flowers of France are much sweeter, but I myself miss the spiciness of the blooms of Scotland. I can remember them. No one believes me but I can!

I read about a bird once — the cuckoo — who lays its eggs in another bird's nest. When the eggs hatch they are raised by that other bird. I sometimes wonder if those birds ever miss their mothers as I do. I miss mine terribly. It has been two years, three months, and ten days since I last saw her. She came for a visit from Scotland then. It was the first time I had seen her since I had left. She gave me a locket with her portrait, which I wear around my neck. I miss her most on my birthday. It is often why I like to be alone — even the day after my birthday. It is why I have come up here to the roof of the château. I have tucked a warm apple pancake wrapped in a handkerchief into my pocket. I miss my mother, but I feel much better up here. Even the Marys know to let me be alone when I come to the roof.

It is a roof garden with immense tubs and pots planted

with shrubs, and in the spring and summer there are flowers. Now the shrubs are all wrapped in heavy cloth, which protects them from the winter cold. They look like little creatures hunched against the sharp wind. I am warm. I have worn the dress of Scotland up here, the tunic, or *leine,* as we call it, this one dyed bright orange and over the *leine* a *brat,* which is a long rectangular piece of wool that is worn as a mantle. On top of it, I drape the pelt of a wolf, which cuts the wind and the cold. The French think this costume most outlandish. "Barbaric," Madame de Parois exclaims whenever she sees me in it. But I like it.

Here in this garden pressed between the sky and the château, I can rest my elbows on the low stone wall at the edge of the roof and look down at the Seine flowing below. It is like a dark satin ribbon in the winter light, and the reflection of the château quivers on its surface. One could almost believe it is unreal — a fairy palace. But it is not. It is made of stone and quite real. And there are no fairy creatures but a squat, angry Queen and a very handsome King and their six children with whom I have played and learned lessons and hawked and skated and danced. Of course some of them are just babies and cannot yet do all that. But we teach one another. Mary Beaton is such a strong, strapping girl that she can even skate with a baby tied to her back. Little Charles loves that. He digs in his tiny heels as if he were a rider on a horse and says giddyap! Mary Beaton just laughs.

DECEMBER 12, 1553

All of us children are so excited. Francis was the first to tell me the wonderful news. He burst into my room this morning, nearly knocking down Minette as she was fixing my hair. "We are to go to Anet!" he shrieked. And then Princess Claude and Princess Elizabeth came running in, squealing with delight. Anet is just about our favorite place to go. It is our favorite because it is the château of Diane de Poitiers, the King's mistress. Diane is the loveliest, most beautiful woman in the world. For all her beauty and elegance she seems to understand children perfectly. She is not young — she is near fifty years — but she can play with us as if she were twelve years old. She thinks up the most wonderful games — contests and treasure hunts with clues.

"Why?" I shouted. "Why ever are we going to Anet? I thought we were supposed to be going directly to Château Blois to join the King and Queen for holidays."

"We shall but not directly," Elizabeth said. "There is

sickness on that route so we must go by way of Anet. It will be safer."

"What will the Queen say?" I asked.

Francis raised his spindly shoulders and turned his palms toward the sky as if to ask how I could be so dense. "Would she want us to die? Better to expose us to Diane de Poitiers than to disease." We all laughed because we know that in Catherine de Medici's mind, Diane is almost as bad as a disease.

DECEMBER 13, 1553
ROYAL BARGE ON THE SEINE EN ROUTE TO ANET

We left before daybreak and I have been out on the deck the entire time. It is chilly, but I carry my muff and I carry Puff in it. Yes, the dear little lapdog that Aunt Anne gave me fits in with just her pink nose sticking out. I can feel her little heart beating on my fingertips. I love this time on the river. I like to watch the night sky grow thin and pale as its darkness turns to gray. They wouldn't let Francis stay on deck, as they fear he's coming down with a sniffle or worse yet, ague. It is terrible when he gets the ague. One minute he is shivering cold and the next he is sweating, and it gives him terrible cramps in his legs. But Princess Elizabeth keeps me company, along with three of the four Marys. Mary Fleming is a lazybones and would never rise before the sun. We are all writing in our diaries. Princess Elizabeth is eight but very mature for eight. She wants to be like the big girls, so beside me she writes in a diary. She keeps asking us how to spell words.

LATER

I was so excited about going to Anet and seeing dear Diane again that I forgot to tell you even more exciting news. Before my uncles left, it was decided that I should have my own household! When talk first came of this a few months ago, I was nervous. I thought it meant that I would never be able to see the royal children. That I would have a house or château apart, I mean, rather like Diane de Poitiers. King Henry is always fixing up a new château for her. She is with us only sometimes. But this is not the same. It really means that I shall have my own domestic staff, and it shall be paid for by the treasury of Scotland. My uncles think that I am treated shabbily or, more to the point, that Queen Mother treats me so. But I am told that there is a good chance that I can add not only a laundress but also an usher of the chamber. This will help me greatly in planning entertainments. And I certainly intend to do so. I am going to give my own *petit bals* and lots of hunting weekends and dinner parties. And I'll get to decide on everything from food for the dinner parties to the decorations. I must hire a good pastry chef. I think I shall give some skating and hawking parties, too. I hope my mother will allow me to choose Master Rufflets as my usher. For although he is quite ancient, he is kind and good. In fact I named my falcon after him — I just dropped the *t*. So the bird is Ruffles.

December 14, 1553
Château d'Anet

I am so tired I can hardly write. But it feels so good to be here, and to arrive on a moonwashed night into the loving arms of our Diane is heaven — pagan heaven, I daresay. Although Diane is a most devout Catholic, her symbols are those of the Greek hunting goddess for whom she is named: Diane, goddess of the hunt and of the moon. As we approached, our excitement mounted. Even the babies, Charles and little Henry, were squealing. We all tried to be the first one to spot the glints of the stag's horns. For indeed, perched on the very top of the entrance arch to the château is a magnificent stone stag with immense antlers. A hound flanks him on either side. All of Anet is made of

Vernon stone, which is white with traces of jet black — the colors of Diane de Poitiers. On this moonlit night the château shimmered with an intensity that took our breath away. Suddenly we all fell silent as we caught sight of Diane. She was standing in the portal of the arch in a dress of white embroidered with silver crescents. Her sleek greyhound dogs were at her feet. Her skin was luminous in the moonlight. I think a little gasp caught in every single one of our throats — even the babies'. She is so unlike any earthly lady.

Diane is the only woman in the French court who wears no cosmetics. Her skin is so white she needs no powders and there is just a tint of pink, but she owes it not to rouge. There are always rumors about Diane's beauty secrets. Some call it an "infernal" and "magical" beauty and speak of witchcraft, of soups made of liquid gold and strange drugs. Some say she bathes in ass's milk. I, however, know the secret and I try to follow it as best I can, although I get lazy sometimes. The secret is icy cold water. She bathes in it every day, sometimes even twice a day. And she pursues vigorous exercise. In court, people bathe perhaps once or twice a month, no more. Queen Catherine thinks it a silly waste of time, so she forbids me to follow Diane's example. But now that I have my own household and staff, I intend to do so. Diane is nearly fifty and she looks hardly twenty, whereas Queen Catherine is much younger and looks over fifty. I must go to sleep now for I intend to be up early to bathe in cold water with Diane and then join her for a ride through the park and woodlands.

P.S. Diane loves Puff even though Puff is not her kind of dog. Diane is partial to her greyhounds.

DECEMBER 16, 1553

How I wish we could stay with Diane forever. That indeed would be the best Christmas present of all. It is as if time were suspended here. We children are truly the center of her attention, and that makes us the most important people in the Château d'Anet. She reads the reports from our tutors carefully and knows about all of our individual progresses.

Diane knows, for example, that Francis and I and Mary Livingston excel in Latin and Greek and Scriptures, but that we are having some difficulty with fractions — adding and subtracting them. She devised the cleverest method for showing us exactly how to add fractions. She cut a piece of paper into a tart shape and then made slices of the tart. She made us add or subtract one-quarters and then subtract or add one-eighths; or perhaps we would deal with thirds and eighths, mixing different fraction bases, which we could never do before. But she explained perfectly the whole of it about common denominators, and after we had worked very diligently, she gave a signal and her usher Monsieur Benoit entered with a real apple tart still warm from the oven. We did the rest of our fractions by cutting the tart.

Even before we had our fraction lessons, Diane and I had been riding for three hours. Francis could not come because of his sniffle. She gave me the big chestnut mare to ride for the first time ever. She said I had grown so tall and my legs were now long enough that I could sit well in the saddle. The four Marys came along with us. They are all excellent riders. You see, we spent much time when we were wee in Scotland riding the small Scottish ponies that are so perfect for young children. Diane was beautiful on her black mare, Jais. She always wears a white riding costume with chiffon veils. And she rides hard and fast like a man. The white of her costume swirls over the blackness of the mare. It is like following one of the funnel-shaped clouds that I have heard about that can spout from the sea or whirl over a flat plain.

December 17, 1553

This afternoon I explored Anet. So much has been done to it since we were last here. The King gave Diane the money to begin restoring the beautiful old château that had belonged to her husband, who died many years ago. They have been fixing and building for nearly seven years! The most famous architect in France, Philibert de'l'Orme, has made the new design. The best craftsmen from all over Europe have come here to sculpt statues, to carve wood panels, to paint gilt ceilings, and to etch glass. On every door and gate there is the royal cipher, one that Henry invented. It is two *D*s with their curves interlocking and joined by a crossbar; thus they lace together to make the letters *D* and *H* for Diane and Henry. It is fitting, for although Henry rules France, Diane reigns supreme within the heart of the King. Queen Catherine, however, chooses to believe that the *D*s are really *C*s. Thus she sees *her* name linked with Henry's. Perhaps it is best for all that she go on believing this. But we know better.

Our time at Anet was much too short. I think of it now like a streak in the sky, a comet flashing through the night. That is always of course how I think of Diane. Black and white and silvery, she sparkles constantly on the edge of my brain. And is it not interesting that the King's guard have a special code name for Diane — Silvius? It fits her perfectly. This is my finest memory of Anet: The last morning we were there I rose early to meet with Diane in the courtyard before our ride. We always meet to wash our faces in the special buckets that she has her chamber-maids set out each evening with rainwater collected from the cistern. This last morning when we arrived there was a skim of ice on the water. I hesitated. "It's the best!" cried Diane, and she plunged her hands into the bucket, crack-ing the ice and splashing the water on her face. She raised her head, eyes sparkling, cheeks wet and glistening. "Es tu timide d'un peu glace, Marie? Are you afraid of a little ice, Mary?" she asked, and I plunged my whole head into the bucket. I heard her roar of laughter even as the water gushed into my ears! I guard this memory as if it were a precious gemstone. I need such memories to survive the court here at Blois. Sometimes, however, I must confess that loving Diane makes me miss my mother even more. It is almost as if I feel guilty about our fun. I think of Mother alone without me in her stony castle in Scotland. I want to write Mother about the things Diane and I do, but then I think this will make her sad and then I get sad just thinking about it. Must rush off. Will write more later.

LATER

Here at Blois there is a stink and all seems dirty compared to Anet, and above the stink there is something worse: the sweet perfume of Queen Catherine. It precedes her wherever she goes. I smell it now. She is coming. Her courtiers scurry ahead like little rodents. I hear the *scritch scratch* of their elegantly booted feet. Their boots are made from the skin of unborn calves. It is an Italian fashion. The Italians love their leather, and of course Catherine de Medici is Italian and was born into what was thought to be a noble family. And yes, I hear as well the *tap tap* of her own high-heeled shoes. Catherine de Medici always wears high heels because she is so short. Then a voice pricks the air. *Tap tap, scritch scratch, yap yap.* That is the "music" of Catherine de

Medici. I always count to eight before I let my old Rufflets open the door. One, two, three . . . The Queen's own lapdogs, of which there are nearly a dozen, yap at my door.

Aah! She has left.

The Queen was accompanied by a few of her retinue of Italians, including Signore Cosmo Ruggieri, trailing along in the sickly sweet wake he created. You see, Ruggieri is her perfumer. But he is not just a perfumer like Signore René the Florentine, the other gentleman who creates scents for the Queen. Ruggieri is also skilled in the ancient arts of alchemy. Through his knowledge of chemistry, he transmutes base metals into precious ones like gold. But it is only his perfume of which we have evidence. He has laboratories here at Blois and also at the Louvre Palace in Paris. They are connected by a secret tunnel to the Queen's apartments, for Queen Catherine insists that the formulas he uses for her perfume be held in complete secrecy.

There are rumors that he makes more than perfume for the Queen. Queen Catherine's name has forever been twined with that of poison, and here at Blois, in the

Queen's apartments, there is a room known as the Queen's cabinets with 237 carved panels along the walls. Four of these have secret cupboards for her jewels and state papers, but some say one is used for poisons. You see, it has for many years been rumored that Catherine de Medici poisoned the King's older brother, who was the eldest son of old King Francis I. By killing him she cleared the way for her husband, Henry, to become king. Many believe it is not just a rumor, but the truth. Furthermore, the Italians are known for their great knowledge of very subtle poisons.

Signore Ruggieri has the complexion of a man whose face has never seen the light of day or felt the wind on his cheeks. Indeed the man reminds me of a candle. His skin is waxy with a yellowish cast and his nose drips off his face like melting tallow. He is too frightening and makes all our skins crawl, even Mary Beaton, who fears nothing. After the Queen and her courtiers leave there is always an awful stillness in the room. Within minutes of the Queen's taking leave, Mary Livingston made up the most wicked rhyme about Queen Catherine. I'll write it down here:

> *Catherine de Medici, plump and squat,*
> *tells us what is*
> *and what is not.*

With her alchemist she dabbles in fate,
arranging destinies,
dispensing hate.

The rhyme gave me a real start, I daresay. I looked into Mary Livingston's wide gray eyes that remind me always of clear pools of water and said, "Do you think it's really true?"

"What, Your Majesty?" she asked, suddenly looking alarmed.

"The part about destiny and hate."

She laughed quickly. "Oh, Mary, they are just words. You know my silly mind just loves to play with words."

But I don't think Mary Livingston really knows the power of her own words.

DECEMBER 21, 1553

I am amazed. I knew I had grown taller this year because none of my clothes fit, and that is why I had a new ball gown made, but I did not realize how tall until I went to the grand ball tonight and danced. Everyone looked short to me — even the King! I was partnered in a pavane first with Monsieur d'un Humaniers, and I looked down onto the small, perfectly round bald patch in the middle of his head. In my bare feet without the heels of my satin slippers, I would be of the same level.

Francis was not allowed to dance any of the fast dances like the galliard. The Queen did not want him to exert himself. However, he did a fine job with the pavanes and the minuets. Francis is not a natural dancer, but pavanes are so easy. Little Mary Seton looked most glorious in the old cloth of silver dress that I had outgrown. I saw Madame de Parois eyeing her, however. She always resents anything I give to the four Marys. She calls them the Savages. She firmly believes that anything from Scotland is rough, wild, and barbaric. We don't care what she thinks.

DECEMBER 22, 1553

The best Christmas surprise of all! Ronsard is back! He had been ailing, and we had missed him so at Saint-Germain. But now he is here! Pierre de Ronsard is the finest poet in France and my favorite tutor. We get on so well. There should be a word that describes the kind of sparkle that happens between two good friends. It is as if we have been friends forever, and indeed Ronsard is the only Frenchman in the French court here who has <u>ever</u> been to Scotland. Yes, indeed before I was born he had been in Scotland and visited the court of my late father, King James V. He more than anybody understands where I come from and to where I shall someday return to rule as Queen. I think about this often. For when Francis and I marry and when he becomes King of France, there will be two thrones that shall need sitting upon. I wonder how we shall divide our time. Well, I shall not worry about that now. I am off to see Ronsard, for if he is here, my lessons continue no matter if it is Christmas.

LATER

It was a pelting icy rain outdoors, but Ronsard and I had a fine time in the library, where it seemed as if the sun were shining. He is quite excited about my having my own household. Of course we worked on Greek poetry. It is his favorite. He tells me of the poems he is writing himself before he tells anyone else. He says I am his confidante. He is devoting himself to perfecting a type of verse in which there are lines of twelve syllables containing four accents. It is very difficult to master. I am not even trying it.

December 24, 1553

These days of Christmas are hard for me. I cannot help but miss my mother more than ever. We begin to fast midafternoon — no evening meal until after Midnight Mass. I grow so hungry, but it is not just my stomach that hungers. It is my heart as well. I think of my mother constantly. I do not know whether to place her at Stirling Castle or Linlithgow. I sense, however, that she might be at the priory on the island of Inchmahome on the north shore of Lake Mentieth. It is only a few hours on horseback from Stirling. It was where they took me after the Scots were defeated at the Battle of Pinkie Cleugh by the English. I was hidden for three weeks. I can almost recall it although I was only four. But I do remember Janet Sinclair waking me up in the middle of the night and telling me — her face a bit too bright, her gray eyes darting nervously — that we were going on an exciting journey. And then I remember the mist on the lake and the monks who seemed to melt out of the mist as our boat approached the shore. The prior himself picked me up in his arms, and it is said I touched his nose and asked why it was so long!

So I try now on this Christmas Eve to fill my stomach and my heart with these memories. I must reach far back to a time that is so dim, to a place that is so distant, and a fine mist that wraps it all. I wonder if the fog will ever lift and if Mother and I shall stand in the sunshine together.

P.S. Francis just paid a visit. He said he wishes we were not considered too old to set out *sabots,* the wooden shoes we sometimes wear for rough play, for Père Noël to put gifts in. But we are! Christmas Eve is quite grim if you're not quite a grown-up but not really a child anymore. Oh, we are given gifts, but serious gifts. Francis is worried that he shall get a sword his father once carried and that it will be too heavy for him and that he shall be embarrassed. He pictures himself falling over under the weight of the sword.

DECEMBER 25, 1553

I am still awake. I have not slept since Midnight Mass. I have been trying to compose a poem — not about Mass. No, about the Orangerie. Christmas Eve held a wonderful surprise. Usually after Mass we all go to the grand salon for *réveillon,* a midnight supper. We are all so hungry that we hurry to the table that is spread with wonderful food. Always a goose gilded in gold leaf, and oysters glistening in their shells, and always a bird with chestnuts. But best of all the Christmas log, *bûche de Noël*, which is a cake rolled up like a log and filled with sweet cream and covered all over with chocolate frosting and silver sugar drops. But this year Ronsard beckoned for Francis and me and the four Marys to follow him. We were all starving, but we went anyway.

He took us to the Orangerie. It is a glass house attached to the south wing of the château. Inside, nearly one hundred orange trees and some lemon ones grow throughout the winter warmed by the sun's heat that is trapped under the glass. It is always exciting to visit in the middle of winter when all the trees outside are bare and there is not a speck of color on the land. Tonight it was utterly magical, for outside it was snowing. Immense flakes drifted down in lazy dances, and if you stood in the darkness of the Orangerie illuminated only by a curve of the moon, it seemed as if you were caught in a rare place. I became part of the night, inseparable from the snow-swirled darkness and the light of the moon, and the oranges suspended and shining. I forgot my hunger. I forgot my sadness. I did not miss my mother for the first time all day. I just wanted to be here. So now I am trying to make it all into a poem. It is so hard.

December 26, 1553

We played games all day long. This is the King's favorite amusement during holidays. He likes for us children to have no lessons and just play. First we played Brittany skittles. It is the best and most complicated game of skittles. Diane, who arrived the night before, is actually awful at this game, and the Queen with Francis can beat her handily. Therefore the Queen was in quite a good mood and wanted to keep playing.

The sun came out brilliantly, and the servants brought us hot chocolate to drink outside. There is nothing better than drinking hot chocolate with one's feet in the snow. Francis then said we must play blindman's buff. I didn't think this was a good idea. Why? The King always cheats, and he peeks in a very sly way through the blindfold and manages to catch Diane. They tumble down to the ground together as if this were the most hilarious thing in the world, and then the Queen gets terribly angry. This is exactly what happened. Sometimes adults really behave stupidly. So then the game was quickly over and we all went inside. That was of course very boring. So Francis, who is very good at thinking up things to do, said we should play a no-grown-ups-allowed game. In other words, one we know they would hate. So we did. *Comme vous allez mourir,* or How will you die? Whoever is It gets to choose a famous figure to be and a pretend weapon to use. Francis always chooses Charlemagne and I always choose to be William Wallace — Braveheart, as he was called. He is my favorite Scottish hero, and he defeated the English King Edward I, who had the nerve to declare himself King of Scotland. The idea of the game is to see who can die the best, the most dramatically. We all play, including Elizabeth and Claude, and we let the babies fool around but they are really too young to judge who dies best. We usually insist that Minette join in although she hates it, and Francis's horse groom, and one or two of the younger footmen. I die spectacularly. I have a way of flopping my body to the ground that makes it look as if it breaks in half. Francis is not nearly as good. It always looks as if he is afraid of bruising himself when he falls. Mary Seton is good at dying, too, although she has a much different style from me. She does a rather slow crumble. Very effective.

DECEMBER 27, 1553

Oh dear, Francis did bruise himself! And played much too hard yesterday. By evening he was too sick and feverish to attend the Saint Stephen's Day feast. Janet Sinclair was not feeling well either, so she did not attend. Saint Stephen's Day is one of my favorite celebrations of the twelve days of the Christmas season. But it just wasn't the same this year — not without Janet and Francis. The King indulged Queen Catherine in her favorite dance of all, the tarantella. It is a very odd and very wild dance that began in the Queen's country of Italy. For such a squat, plump woman she does the tarantella with great grace.

During a rest between dances, I was sitting near the Queen, and Diane de Poitiers came up to her and in her kind and gentle way implored that the Queen not dance so hard.

"Do not concern yourself, my dear!" Queen Catherine said. "You now how well I do at this point always." I could not make out what she meant but she seemed appreciative of Diane's concern, though Diane still seemed worried.

I asked the Queen if I might not take some of the zabaglione in a silver cup to Francis in his chambers. She pinched my cheek and said, "Yes, little one. You are so gentle with Francis. What a fine wife you will make."

"I am a good friend now," I replied.

"Yes," she answered, and I could not read all that was in her eyes. I simply hate it when people talk about me and Francis being married. The four Marys know never to mention this to me. I have promised them that nothing will change once I am married. They will still remain in court as my ladies-in-waiting, my best friends, whether we are in Scotland or France.

DECEMBER 28, 1553

Oh dear, everything is upside down. Queen Catherine has suffered a miscarriage. Now I know why Diane was so concerned. She did dance too hard. I had no idea that the Queen was with child. Diane is always the first to know. She always arranges for the midwife and the wet nurse. It is very odd, because although the Queen is jealous of Diane and considers her an enemy in her own affections for the King, she knows that, above all, Diane has the best interests of the King at heart. And the best interests of the King are identical to those of the Queen — their children.

LATER

I visited with Francis this afternoon. I was told not to tell him about the Queen's miscarriage. I think it is absolutely rotten when adults keep information from children, but I shall do as I am told. I distracted Francis by having him help me plan my first entertainment, now that I have an independent household and much more money to spend. I plan to give a dinner at midday on the first day of the new year. My uncles de Guises are to attend and of course the four Marys. I did not tell Francis but I am more than relieved that the Queen will most likely be unable to attend. Mostly Francis and I talked about the food. I told him there will be zabaglione. I am engaging an Italian chef. There is no doubt about it, Queen Catherine has brought new tastes to the French court, and the best chefs are Italian. They know how to use herbs. At least that is what everyone says. Of course how should I know, being just a rough Scot raised on haggis and all. Mary Livingston says I should give a special luncheon and invite Madame de Parois and have my chef cook haggis. I told her that my chef would quit my service. You see, haggis is a bit of a barbarian dish but we Marys love it. It is a kind of stew made from beef liver and heart and lamb kidneys all chopped up and then boiled with oatmeal in the bladder of a cow. It sounds terrible but it is really very good. One serves it with what we Scots call neeps and tatties, or turnips and potatoes. The French would hate it.

DECEMBER 31, 1553

Last day of the old year. As is the custom of my mother, I have fasted today and have now sought audience with my private confessor, Father Mamerot. The problem is that with my stomach empty I think of my mother more. I hunger not so much for food but for Mother. I remember, though it was long ago, fasting with her.

The fast helps cleanse my mind of *les petits vanities,* the little vanities, and *les choses legere,* or trivial things. I know exactly what my mother means. I put out of my mind thoughts of gold ball gowns and mean notions that do not become my station. I must try to divert my mind from all meanness and baseness and not take delight in Mary Livingston's tart, saucy rhymes. I must try to have a better attitude toward Queen Catherine. I also plan to have a very serious talk with the four Marys. Together we must make vows not to delight in ridicule and try to see the best in people such as Madame de Parois. I must take the lead in guiding the Marys. For indeed I am their Queen, and it is the moral and divine duty of a Queen to cultivate a garden in which higher moral thoughts might take root. So now I have all this organized in my mind. I shall immediately seek Father Mamerot.

I am so mad at Queen Catherine and Madame de Parois. I hope Mary Livingston does make up some absolutely livid rhymes for those two! Now I know why Janet Sinclair did not come to the Saint Stephen's Day celebration! Now I know why she has not been to the grand salon but a few times this entire holiday season. It is because Queen Catherine, undoubtedly at Madame de Parois's urging, has given great offense to my dear nurse, my darling Janet Sinclair. Unbeknownst to me, that cheap merchant's daughter had reduced Janet Sinclair's and her husband, John Kemp's, allowance for wine and kindling and candles in their apartments.

I fear that even though I am now in charge of my own household these differences between Catherine de Medici and myself will sharpen. The differences began long ago. I remember when I first came here it was Diane de Poitiers who greeted me and the four Marys. She curtsied and called me "Your Majesty" and brimmed with what my mother would call the *les vrais gentillesses,* the true refinements of a great lady. It was several days before the King and Queen arrived. Then this scowling, pudgy lady raced into the nursery. I did not know who she was and was shocked when I realized it was indeed Francis's mother. She did not even greet me at all. So I drew myself up and said exactly who I was — in French at that. I had learned only a few words. So I said, "Madame la Reine, Vous connaissez ques vous êtes en la presence d'une Reine? Je suis la Reine d'Ecosse. (Madame Queen, do you know that you are in the presence of a queen? I am the Queen of Scots.)"

Catherine countered by asking whether I realized that I ("little saucy one," as she called me) was in the presence of the Queen of France.

The fact is, there simply is not room for two queens in one country, let alone in one palace.

JANUARY 3, 1554

The other Marys are just as mad as I am at Queen Catherine, and they forgive my talk to them of the other day, when I sought to guide them away from ridicule and to higher moral thoughts. Mary Livingston wants to know if she can make up nasty poems once more. I said fine. It is nothing compared with taking away one's kindling and candles, depriving them of warmth and light!

But then Mary Fleming, who is a timid, cautious sort,

said, "Be careful, Mary Livingston. We do not want Queen Catherine going to her cabinet." A shiver went through us all. The word "poison" hung in the air unspoken.

JANUARY 4, 1554

Well, I am a cuckoo no more. This is definitely my nest that I am feathering. I have two new pages and two new *valets de chambres*. They are really to help with service in the four Marys' apartments, and needless to say the four Marys are in ecstasy. Now they shall be able to have their own card parties and have their guests served properly. I am allowing one of the new pages to run messages and announce just for the Marys. I also have a *maître de hôtel*, a Monsieur Jallet, who shall take care of ordering all my household goods from food to firewood. Janet Sinclair says I must go through all my clothes and gowns and see what is worn out and what I have outgrown. Mary Fleming is the tiniest of the four Marys, and I shall give to her all those clothes that are still perfect but too small. The others I shall distribute among the three other Marys so they can give them to their favorite servants. This will annoy Madame de Parois to no end, for she likes to give them to her closest friends in exchange for favors and sometimes she even sells them.

January 5, 1554

Puff gave birth to two little puppies this morning! They are no bigger than thimbles! The four Marys and I are so excited. We fear, however, that Puff might not have enough milk. I have sent Monsieur Jallet to search out a wet-nurse dog for our puppies. He looked a bit surprised but went off cheerfully.

Later

No wet-nurse dog yet, but Mary Beaton had a very good idea. We are taking embroidery thread and dipping it into bowls of milk and then letting the two little "thimbles" suck.

JANUARY 6, 1554

Alas, one little thimble died last night just after we came back from the midnight banquet for Twelfth Night. To think that while we were dancing and listening to minstrels and watching jugglers, the little pup was gasping his last. We are planning a funeral. How sad — my second entertainment as head of my own household is to be a funeral. I sent word to Father Confessor Mamerot to meet us in *Les Champs du Repos*, the pet cemetery here at Blois.

JANUARY 7, 1554

Because of the funeral the four Marys and Francis and Elizabeth and Claude and I decided to delay giving our Twelfth Night presents. So we did it this morning when we had our hot chocolate. I had embroidered small purses for the four Marys, which they loved. For Princesses Elizabeth and Claude I had embroidered small covers for their books from which they shall begin their studies of Greek and Latin. But the best gift that I gave was for Francis. It, too, was a book with an embroidered cover but filled with blank pages. On the very first page I had written in beautiful gilt script, almost as good as the royal calligrapher, the words *Le Registre de la Chasse du Dauphin, Francois,* The Record of the Hunt of the Dauphin, Francis. It is a book for him to record his successes when hunting. Francis loves to hunt and has already killed two wild boars, which is very good for someone who is not even eleven and of such a frail constitution. But he is an excellent horseman and superb with the bow. As a wonderful surprise the King arrived and gave each of us a present, including a lovely sapphire pendant for me that is encircled with pearls. He also, and I felt this was so kind, extended his sympathies for the little pup and asked to see how the other one is doing. Quite well, I am pleased to say. We have named him Thimble.

January 9, 1554

We prepare to go to Paris, the Louvre Palace. It is not one of our favorite places, but the happy news is that we shall be there only awhile and then shall go to Château Chambord in the Loire Valley, which indeed is one of our favorite places and where Francis's and my best horses are. His two are Fontaine and Enghiene, and mine are Bravane and Madame la Reale. There will be hunting for two weeks or more and then on to Chenonceau, another favorite château of ours, where there is usually good ice skating.

January 10, 1554

It is said that the reason we are rushing off to Paris is because Queen Catherine seeks a new astrologer. She is disenchanted with Ruggieri for he had predicted a robust, healthy baby boy before she miscarried. There is talk of another astrologer who is supposed to have immense powers of prediction. He is known as Nostradamus, and it has been arranged for him to be at the Louvre Palace. They even say that he shall occupy the old observatory. That indeed would make him the Queen's First Astrologer. If Michel Nostradamus can make perfume, Ruggieri will certainly be out of a job.

January 11, 1554

A corsetier has come to take my measurements for new hoops. All of my vasquines seem to have collapsed. They can no longer do the task for which they were made — to expand my skirts. The fabric pools on the floor and nearly causes me to trip, so eight new ones have been ordered. They are to be made with well-tempered metal. Also, we found that although we had checked my gowns, we had forgotten about my shoes. I have outgrown many or danced the soles off. We have ordered ten new pairs. Janet says I cannot wear high heels anymore since I have grown so tall. I love high heels. They sparkle so when one dances, as the cobblers embed small jewels in the heels. I also need some new gloves. I have asked that they be embroidered with harebells and thistle designs, the flowers of my native land.

JANUARY 17, 1554
LE LOUVRE PALACE, PARIS

Master Clouet the court painter is here working on royal portraits of Princess Elizabeth and Princess Claude. He is so nice to all of us children and always finds time to help us with our drawing. I have decided to do a portrait of Puff and Thimble, and he will help me, he says.

We have heard much about this man Nostradamus. Francis has actually met him and says he is much nicer than Ruggieri. He is a Jew. I do not think I have ever met a Jew. And Francis says he truly has the eyes of a seer. I ask what he means. He says that I must see them for myself. The man's eyes are beyond description. The four Marys and I are so eager to meet him. Queen Catherine is having him make astrological charts for all her children. I hope he doesn't say anything about the date when I am to marry Francis. I really do not want to hear anything about that right now.

January 18, 1554

My uncles have arrived to discuss important business with King Henry. It concerns the signing of vital papers that would make my mother the Queen Regent in Scotland until I am eighteen years old — old enough to rule by myself.

King Henry has consulted with me about the talks with my uncles. Yes, he came to me just as he would an older ruler. My mother had advised me in a letter I received soon after I got here of her desire to officially make King Henry my guardian along with my uncles de Guises. I must sign these guardian papers before my mother can become my Regent, the person who rules in Scotland while I am a child. The King explained to me just what his guardianship will mean. He is to look after my well-being, ensure that I am well guarded at all times — for indeed when I was nine years old there was a plot to poison me! He also will continue to choose my tutors. But we both know it is really Diane who does that. I practiced signing my name all morning before he came because I would hate to dribble ink in some unseemly fashion on such important documents.

LATER

The papers are not to be signed yet for some weeks. There is possibly a problem with Lord Arran, I believe. He is also called the Duke of Châtelherault. He is a Lord Governor of the Scottish estates and represents Scotland in France. He at one time hoped that his son would be my bridegroom. Thank heavens that is not to be, for his son is simpleminded.

JANUARY 19, 1554

I have at last met Nostradamus. Francis is right. The man's eyes are indescribable. I expected them to be very dark with piercing glints, but they are a mild gray, and when you look into them they suggest the vastness of the sky. No, not just the sky — the entire cosmos, the firmament and the stars. There is both heaven and earth in those eyes and maybe hell. But he is kindly and has a gentle way. His beard is long. He has a broad forehead, a straight nose, and steadiness of expression — unlike Ruggieri who has a special look for the Queen, and then what the four Marys and I call his look for children — a mincing smile and a too-sweet voice. I do not like people who have one way of speaking to adults and another to children.

We were visiting the Queen's apartments. There were several of us — Francis, the four Marys, and all the babies with their nursemaids. Both dance masters were there, Monsieur de Rege and the ballet master, Monsieur Balthazar. Queen Catherine has plans for us to learn a ballet. The visit was quite merry, with lots of cakes and glazed tarts. The babies were whirling about like little spinning tops and at least a dozen lapdogs were yapping. Queen Catherine was in a very fine mood. She did not mind the wildness, the confusion of spilled cups, barking dogs, and flying cake crumbs. Princesses Claude and Elizabeth and I were chasing the babies with feather fans, playing a tickle game that Claude had invented and the babies loved. Nostradamus was sitting close to the Queen, and they were regarding us in the game. She was pointing first to Charles, then Elizabeth, and so on. I was not paying much attention, but the four Marys were near, and suddenly I saw them all grow quite still. Mary Fleming, the most delicate, turned a ghastly white. I thought she might faint. I quickly went up to them. "What is wrong?"

"Nothing!" Mary Beaton said suddenly. "Nothing at all!" She grabbed my feather fan and began chasing little Henry and Claude. It was bedlam. Shrieks of laughter. But I was left wondering. Why did my Marys look so odd? What had Nostradamus whispered to the Queen?

JANUARY 20, 1554

I am still unsettled by the four Marys' behavior. They seemed false with me at supper tonight, as if they were trying too hard at merriment. I know they are hiding something from me. I shall go to Mary Seton and ask her. She is an honest and direct sort. Indeed she did not join in the false gaiety tonight but remained very quiet.

JANUARY 21, 1554

Last night before retiring for bed I went to Mary Seton's chambers. She was almost ready for bed. Her chamber-maid Violette, whom she shares with Mary Livingston, was surprised to see me and Mary even more so.

"What brings you here?" Mary asked, adjusting her nightcap.

I walked right up to her as she stood by her bed and took both her hands in mine and held them firmly. She looked down at her feet in the embroidered night slippers, as if the flowers stitched of blue- and rose-colored beads were the most interesting things in the world. I laughed softly. "Even in silence you cannot tell a lie, can you, Mary Seton?" Her fingers tightened in my hands. "Look at me, Mary Seton." My voice was gentle, but it was the command of a Queen to her subject. She would not refuse. Her steady blue eyes looked into mine. They brimmed with tears! "Mary dear, what is it? What did Nostradamus say?"

"Oh, Milady. It cannot be true. Of this I am sure."

"Just tell me, Mary, and let me be the judge."

Mary Seton lifted her chin and looked straight at me. "All the children had been running about and Queen Catherine suddenly said to Nostradamus, 'You have told me of my children, but what about the one from Scotland? Do you perceive any calamity threatening this fair young head?' And he answered in a very low voice, but we four Marys heard. 'Madame,' he said, 'I perceive blood.'" Mary Seton's chin began to quiver, and the tears that brimmed in her eyes fell in silvery tracks down her cheek.

How can I describe my feelings? A terrible blackness seemed to well up from the pit of my stomach. I grasped

Mary Seton's hands harder, but then from someplace within me there came a strange and mysterious strength. I knew that I must not succumb to fear or tremors or tears. I must show courage. The blood of William Wallace does not run in my veins, but indeed his spirit invades my heart. I shall be a Braveheart worthy of Scotland. "Rest your fears, Mary Seton, and tell the other Marys to rest theirs. I shall speak with Monsieur Nostradamus myself. And remember, not every prophecy is fulfilled. Perhaps we should be grateful, for it will make us all the more vigilant."

As this point Mary Seton gasped and fell to her knees. "Your Majesty," she whispered, "you are a true daughter of Scotland. You are bold of heart and stout of mind. You are a Queen!"

"And you four Marys are the most faithful subjects a Queen could ever have."

JANUARY 22, 1554

Tonight I plan to go to Nostradamus's observatory. I know that the Queen makes night visits to him and with him observes the position of the stars. But the Queen will not be there tonight, as it is raining and the sky is thick with clouds and shall be starless. I cannot go alone for I am always to be accompanied by a guard. But whom to take? Monsieur Jallet, my *maître d'hôtel*? A wonderful servant but I fear he can be indiscreet. He loves gossip. My footman Alain — he, too, talks too much with all the grooms in the stables. Rufflets is simply too old. I must think on this. Meanwhile Princess Claude, Princess Elizabeth, Mary Livingston, Mary Fleming, and I are required to go to the music room. Queen Catherine is determined to have ballet master Balthazar teach us a ballet she wants us to learn. I am, needless to say, in no mood for ballet. It amazes me that even though I have my own household and can spend my own money I still am treated as a child in many ways. Janet Sinclair says I must be part of this stupid ballet. It would offend the King if I did not participate. We are to play the roles of ancient prophetesses. Ronsard has composed poetry to be accompanied by music from the rebec, and we are to dance these steps. I do not want to pretend to be some prophetess and dance around in a silly costume. It is so tedious, so boring, and all I want to do is see the prophet Nostradamus.

LATER

I have had an inspired idea. I shall take no one with me to see Nostradamus. I shall disguise myself as a chambermaid. I have already spoken with Minette. We shall trade clothes for an hour or so. I shall put on her coif, partlets, kirtle, and smock, and whatever else a serving maid wears. I suddenly realize I really don't know — at least not about the undergarments.

JANUARY 23, 1554
JUST AFTER MIDNIGHT

I am waiting now until the ancient guard who stands at the end of the corridor leading from my apartments to the grand salon is asleep. If it were young Robin MacClean, one of my Scots guards, I would not have a chance. But as soon as this old goat nods off, I can cross through the grand salon to the petit salon. There is a small passageway from that room that leads to the observatory. I never knew about this passageway, but Minette told me. She says that it is right behind the statue of King Charlemagne. There is a panel that appears ordinary like all the others in the salon but if I push, it will open. She cautions me that the stairs are steep. What an adventure!

Already just getting into Minette's clothes has been an adventure. How different they are and not just in appearance. She wears no undergarments, as least hardly any worth mentioning. There is no corseting and no hoops. No underpinnings or true partlets to fill in the neckline of the bodice or to wear over the kirtle. Well, actually there is no kirtle. She wears a loose shift and then she ties two skirts over that and laces up a vest that is scooped into a squarish neck. Instead of a partlet to hide the skin exposed by the bodice, she tucks in a scarf. Then over the two skirts there is an apron.

Not one of these garments has a stitch of decoration or embroidery. Minette's hair is entirely covered with a soft cap, the kind they call a muffin cap, for it looks as if a muffin or biscuit has plopped down on one's head. But I must wear it or my red hair would reveal me immediately. Meanwhile Minette has slipped into my night rail and my bed and is giggling madly. She says she has never felt anything as lovely as my fine cambric sleeping gown, and I say I have never felt anything as coarse as her carzie wool. I think the sheep this wool came from spent their entire lives in brambles. But now the deepest part of the night comes and Minette says it is safe for me to go. I will take one taper with me. I will go to visit the seer and ask about this blood he sees swirling around my head.

JANUARY 24, 1554

I do not quite know what to make of my meeting with Michel Nostradamus. I traversed the great salon, then went into the small one, where indeed behind the statue of Charlemagne I found the panel. The steps were steep as Minette said, but it was a short distance to the bottom. However, it seemed that I threaded my way forever through the narrow, dark tunnel. I suddenly panicked when the flame of my candle began guttering. I should have brought a second one to light from the first, a tinder flint or striking squib. I think my heart would have stopped if I had had no light. It was a dank and scary place to be. I saw the long thin tail of a rat disappear into a crevice. But finally I got to the end, where I mounted some other steps. These steps wound upward and upward in a spiral, and it seemed as if they, like the tunnel, would never end. To my surprise as I wound round the last bend, a door creaked open. There was a wedge of light, and then a large shadow slid out and printed itself against the stone wall. From the shadow came a voice. "I was expecting you, child." I began to tremble fiercely. "Fear not," he said, and his voice was so warm and kindly, I was drawn to it like the iron filings I once saw pulled to a magnet in a demonstration by Ruggieri.

When I entered the observatory, the doctor, for indeed he is a physician, as I soon learned, was standing beside a tripod that held a brass bowl. I walked directly to it and saw my reflection in the water it held. "What do you see?" he asked.

"My own reflection," I replied. I peered harder, then suddenly tore off my muffin cap. Tendrils of my hair fanned out around my face.

"And now?" he asked.

"Fire. Not blood," I said, and I looked into those eyes of his that held the infinity of the sky.

Francis had told me that Nostradamus gave his predictions in the form of the four-line verses we call quatrains. Now he spoke:

> *Some speak of heaven's dart,*
> *others the symmetry of the rose.*
> *Some of fire, some of blood,*
> *a life without repose.*

"What does it mean?" I asked.

"There is no precise meaning," he replied.

"No real meaning?" I was astounded.

"The meaning is real but not exact. People want everything to be exact. But trust me when I say that the inexact, the imprecise, is no less real than the exact and the precise."

"Then it could be blood that swirls around my head, or it could be the petals of a rose — perhaps the red rose of the House of Tudor, my English cousins Elizabeth, Mary, and Edward, their father, Henry VIII — or it could be fire?"

"Yes. But there will be tumult, my dear. There will be chaos and confusion, and there will never be complete repose."

"But not necessarily blood."

"Not necessarily." He nodded and his eyes softened.

I thought on all this for a minute, no more. Then I looked up into the kind face of this man. "That is good enough for me. I am a Queen. I expect to have some hand in making my own destiny, and that of my people of Scotland. And thus I do not expect repose."

"You are old beyond your years."

"I have been Queen since I was but nine months old. I have been separated from my mother since I was five, betrothed to a lovely but weak lad since I was four. I have been the cuckoo bird in a very strange nest. Yes, it does make one old beyond one's years."

And I turned and left the good man. Left him to his

tripod and his bowl of water with its reflections of clouds and stars and red-haired girls who were Queens before their time. I threaded my way back through the tunnels, and indeed my candle did gutter out and I was left in total darkness. I felt myself absorbed into the night. I heard the scutterings of running rats and I might have even heard the *tap tap* of those high-heeled shoes of the merchant's daughter, but I was not fearful for I am a Queen, a true Queen. I ripped off my servant's muffin cap and let my hair stream out like rays of sun.

JANUARY 26, 1554

I waited until today to tell the four Marys of my visit. They were stunned. "You went there by yourself?" Mary Beaton gasped.

"What did he say?" asked Mary Fleming, her delicate face beautiful and quivering like a small flower in a summer breeze. So I told the Marys all about it. They remained silent for a long moment. Then Mary Beaton dropped on one knee. "Your Majesty, your courage inspires us. I vow that I shall remain by your side whatever the tumult, wherever fortunes good or ill take you, and mostly, although I know you do not like talk of marriage, I vow never to marry before you."

"Aye . . . Aye . . . Aye." There was a soft chorus of ayes, and the three other Marys dropped to their knees and vowed as well to follow me through tumult and repose and never to marry until I have so done. Did any person have a luckier charm than these four steadfast friends? They are my clover leaf for eternity.

JANUARY 27, 1554

We leave for Chambord tomorrow. I must finish my Greek translation of the Anacreon poems for Ronsard. Then I am to try my own hand at writing one in the same meter. I am looking forward to going to Chambord. Francis is beside himself, so excited is he to see once more his favorite horses. The only problem is that it is so complicated whenever the court moves to a different château. There is much packing up to do, and now that I have my own household I must confer with my *maître d'hôtel*, Monsieur Jallet, for hours over what seems like a thousand and one details. We need additional carriages now that we are an independent household, for our servants must ride separately. Some of course ride on horseback, but Rufflets and Monsieur Jallet need their own conveyances. I think they might ride together in one. We also need to provide for an assistant for Madame Moillard, the seamstress. So many new gowns have been ordered for me that she cannot take on all the work in addition to her duties for Queen Catherine. Monsieur Jallet proposed that the assistant ride with the chambermaids, but I don't think this is appropriate. I think women of stitchery believe themselves to be superior to women of the bedchamber, and this could cause problems. Madame de Parois has demanded her own carriage. Simply ridiculous! There is so much to think about, and all I want to do at this moment is please Ronsard with my translation. I think I shall invite him to ride in my carriage with me to Chambord. Unfortunately, Diane de Poitiers has gone back to Anet for a while. I hope she comes to Chambord for there is such fun to be had there — the hunting and hawking, and there is talk of a very grand ball.

FEBRUARY 1, 1554
CHÂTEAU CHAMBORD

Arrived last night at twilight. It is the best time to first glimpse Chambord. The entire roof of Chambord can be seen from miles away and almost seems like a chessboard with its countless spires and chimneys that stand like chess pieces bristling against the sky. We have — Francis, Claude and Elizabeth, the four Marys, and myself — tried to count the chimneys. Every time we come up with a different number, but there are well over three hundred, of that we are sure. Chambord is like a world within another world. It is hard to believe that contained within the more than twenty miles of walls there is an immense forest park. The château stands in the center, but the thickets and glades are astir with wolves and wild boar and stag. It is a hunter's paradise. Before dawn one hears the sound of the horns summoning the dogs into the courtyards. Each blast on the horn is a specific signal for the dogs. Of course, Francis likes best to hunt with his falcons and hawks. He keeps a dozen or more here. There is only one problem. Queen Catherine forbids us to hunt tomorrow. It is Candlemas Day, the celebration of the purification of the Virgin Mary, and the day must be spent in devotion. Then there is the Candlemas feast in the evening. Indeed we must begin a fast tonight. I do not think I would object so much if Queen Catherine's form of religion did not seem to me so inconstant. Father Confessor Mamerot despairs over her reliance on sorcerers and seers such as Ruggieri and Nostradamus. He once said to me in an unguarded moment that the Queen, as he put it, "rejects the divine truths of scriptural revelations but believes in these soothsayers and starry messengers." Thus no hunting tomorrow and Francis is very upset. He whines like a baby.

FEBRUARY 2, 1554

Mary Beaton pounced on my bed this morning and shook me. "Up, up! We must get out of doors right now."

"Why?"

"Mary Stuart!" All four Marys gathered round my bed. Now Mary Livingston raised her voice. "Have you forgotten our dear Scotland? It is not all prayers this Candlemas Day and going about with candles."

I smacked my forehead with the sudden realization. Indeed I had forgotten. "Quick, Minette, dress me." Minette came rushing in with my partlets and hoops and corset. Oh, my goodness, I thought. So many layers to put on. I needed to be quick. I remembered the night I visited Nostradamus. How free my body felt in Minette's clothes without all those underpinnings of partlets and corsets. "Minette, I shall not need my corsets or partlets. Yes, and I think I'll not wear a kirtle. Just my chemise and overdress and those heavy, thick stockings."

A silence filled the room. Minette stood with her mouth open. The four Marys looked as if I had gone mad.

"Have you taken leave of your senses?" Mary Seton gasped.

"Of course not, but do you want to get out to the courtyard or not? The sun waits for no one — not even the Queen of the Scots!" I replied.

They all giggled, and quick as a pig dipped in lard I was in my clothes. We roared out of our apartments, which are in the lantern tower. Mary Beaton was singing in Gaelic at the top of her lungs an ancient song sung by old Highland chieftains:

> *Edward Longshanks, Edward Longshanks,*
> *You come to claim our kin.*
> *Our fair land, our fairer folk*
> *You come to slay again.*
>
> *But Braveheart will cut you down*
> *And save our children dear*
> *And banish bloody English troops*
> *For he does not know fear.*

We passed Madame de Parois on the grand double staircase. A look of horror scored her face. "Savages!" she muttered and pressed herself against the ballustrade.

Out in the courtyard we danced about, looking for our shadows and chanting the Scottish rhyme:

> *If Candlemas Day is bright and clear*
> *There'll be two winters in the year.*

And then Mary Livingston made up another verse:

> *And if you see your shadow now*
> *There'll be snow on your favorite cow.*

Janet Sinclair came down and joined us in the court-yard. "Girls, girls! Oh, shadows!" she exclaimed as she saw our dancing ones on the cobbles. "Spring will be here soon!" She joined in our fun and laughed at our antics. But then the dread words: "You must go up now and bathe, girls." We all groaned. "This is the day of the purification of the Virgin. I shan't hear of you not bathing. It has been since Saint Stephen's Day six weeks ago that you had your last bath. Now, go for the honor of the Blessed Virgin."

LATER

After midnight. We fell to the food on the banquet table like ravenous wolves, after fasting all day. Mary Fleming nearly fainted when we walked in procession through the chapel with our lighted candles. That is the custom. This is the part of Candlemas Day I love the most. I wore a dress embroidered all over with silver and pink and violet threads and tiny pearls formed into roses and jasmine and marguerites. To wear the dress was like walking in a garden. On my ears were the double-drop pearl and diamond earrings given to me by my grandmother de Guise. My coif was a masterpiece of whitework embroidery — white linen thread on a white background. I did not want it to glint or shimmer or be studded with jewels. I felt that my headdress should appear humble and most simple, for if the Virgin Mary does look down on me she should not be blinded by the flash of jewels. I come to her humbly with the light of my taper and a bowed head. Queen Catherine and several other women of the court wore their usual court makeup. Some of the Marys tried the whitening pastes for the first time for the banquet afterward, but I came in my own skin and the tint of my own blood and the scroll of the faint blue vein that runs near my temple.

February 3, 1554

Hardly time to write. Francis stamps about impatiently in my receiving salon while I dress in my chamber. We must rush on to see the horses and the dear falcons.

Later

Too tired to write. Hunted and hawked all day. Then went to the archery field and practiced with the larger bows under the instructions of my Scots guardsmen. It is known that the Scots are the best archers. I have been advanced to a larger and heavier bow. Robin MacClean, the head guard, praised me and said that he never saw anyone take to this bow faster. Robin is an excellent teacher. He is a big ruddy fellow with the keenest blue eyes and the burr of the Highlands in his voice. I do feel a little bit bad, for Francis is still on the lighter bow. But the fact is I am a good several inches taller than Francis and such a long bow would be most awkward for him. I do wish Francis would grow! Surely he will grow by the time we marry. He is so short that we would look quite silly as a bride and groom standing in front of the priest exchanging our sacred vows. He barely reaches my shoulder now.

We went hawking again this afternoon but first we had to have lessons. And unfortunately, we had to rehearse that stupid ballet. Queen Catherine watched it all and inter- jected her comments. "Children, you must do as Monsieur Balthazar says." Then she said very grandly, "This is the vocabulary of ballet." And she demonstrated often herself, pointing that plump little foot, holding up that arm with its sagging flesh, and fixing me with her beady eyes as if to challenge me to refuse her direction.

I would rather translate a thousand lines of Latin with my Latin master, George Buchanan, hanging over my shoulder, whose breath always stinks of ale, than do five seconds of that stupid dance. Monsieur Balthazar insists that we turn out our legs in a manner for which our anatomy was not designed. He has these ridiculous posi- tions for us to practice. There is first position, second posi- tion, and so forth. They are excruciatingly difficult and between all the riding I am doing, in addition to the ballet nonsense, my legs feel like forks with the tines pulled apart. I won't give up the riding. And I do not understand why, if I am Queen of Scotland and have my own house- hold and my own treasury from which to buy whatever I want, I have to stand in first position looking like a duck with splayed feet. This is all very Italian. It all came from Florence.

FEBRUARY 5, 1554

I am so excited — no lessons today. Just hunting. The four Marys and I have decided to wear our Scots dress. Oh, we do look savage. The King loves it. The air here at Chambord does something to us.

FEBRUARY 6, 1554

The uncles have arrived. My uncle Francis, le Balafré, talks too much about marriage. And they all inquire incessantly about Francis's health. I can tell them only what I know. I do know that Nostradamus has recommended that Francis take rose pills that are made from the crushed petals of roses and drink lots of rose tea. He says it will protect him from his frequent colds and earaches. And it might be working. Francis's nose, which runs perpetually, seems to have dried up in recent days. I know why my uncles inquire. They fear that Francis might die before we are married and that I shall never have a chance to become Queen of France as well as of Scotland. I suppose it is a problem, but I myself would miss Francis as a friend more than as a husband. I cannot say this to my uncles, and I cannot ask them to stop speaking of marriage. It is amazing the seemingly simple things a Queen is not permitted to do. Sometimes I muse that a plain serving girl like Minette has more freedom than I do. I know she has a suitor — Marcel, a groomsman. And Mary Livingston and Mary Beaton, who seem to know about such things, feel that Minette and Marcel have done a lot of kissing — a lot! They have seen the mark on her neck. Apparently if one kisses another very hard, it leaves a bluish mark on the skin. It is called *la marque.*

FEBRUARY 7, 1554

Spent the morning trying on gowns for tomorrow's ball. An old one I had outgrown is now perfect for Mary Fleming. There is one lovely brocade that no longer fits, and I think I shall give it to the abbess of the nearby convent to make curtains for the chancel, as she so appreciated a bolt of cloth that I donated last year.

LATER

Madame de Parois has been in a most foul humor ever since we have arrived at Chambord. At first I thought it was just our wildness, the way the four Marys and I were tearing about in our Scottish costumes and babbling away in Gaelic, which does sound rough in the throat compared with French. But this afternoon she became absolutely nasty — a scowl etched on her face, snapping at everyone. She even tried to kick little Thimble out of the way. I scooped up Thimble, who was quivering with fear, and I just burst out, "Madame, what is it in you that delights in kicking a dog that weighs no more than a cabbage?"

Madame de Parois then looked over at the dress that I plan to give to the abbess. "I see," she said, "that you are afraid of my enriching myself in your service. It is plain you intend to keep me poor."

"That is not my intention at all, Madame. But why should the church not benefit from this brocade, and Mary Fleming is the perfect size for this other gown of mine. I am sorry this inconveniences you."

FEBRUARY 8, 1554

Ronsard promises he will join me tonight in a pavane. The four Marys and Princess Elizabeth and I are planning to spend this afternoon practicing with cosmetics. Minette and Dora, another chambermaid, will bring the lacquer boxes with the powders and pastes to my boudoir. We all need some whitening, for our skin has become tinted with riding and hawking and spending so much time outdoors. Veils never stay on when one rides as hard as we do.

LATER

What an amusement it has been. The lacquer boxes contain delicate porcelain pots filled with various pastes and powders and creams. We have with Dora's and Minette's help spread a thin layer of the ceruse all over our faces and bosoms. My freckles, which lay in an unseemly band across my nose, are gone! Dora then showed us how to dip a fluffy brush into a small pot of madder. One shakes the brush twice, then dips it into a pot of vermilion. In this way two colors are blended — an ochre and a deep red — and it makes a lovely light blush that we touch onto our cheeks. Mary Livingston has an unsightly spot in the middle of her chin, but Dora fixed up an extra thick paste and now it is as gone as my freckles. Then we painted on lip color.

I think I am going to look very lovely for the ball. I plan to wear the gown that is laced with ribbons of silver. The sleeves are of quilted satin, and I shall carry a feather fan.

FEBRUARY 10, 1554

Disaster — the ball was an utter disaster. I am just now recovering. I bless Doctor Nostradamus. Had it not been for him I do not know what would have happened. I shall try to describe the horrifying event. The first dance as usual was a bransle. Francis and I began the first series of kicks — kick left, kick right. By the end of four kicks, I began to feel a slight prickling sensation on my face. I paid it no heed. But by the end of the dance, I felt a numbness beginning near my jawline. I touched my face lightly for I did not want to disturb the makeup. I felt fine. So I joined another set of dances. By the end of the second set, half of my face felt completely numb, and although numb, my lips and nose felt as if they were hugely fat. I dragged Mary Livingston off to the side. "Is my lip swollen?" I asked.

"What are you talking about?"

I told her that I was having the strangest sensation in my face.

At that moment Monsieur Ronsard walked up. "The pavane?" he said, reminding me of our promised dance together.

"Oh, certainly," I replied, putting the business of my face out of my head. Or so I thought. For to dance with a poet like Ronsard is heaven. His rhythms are so natural even the clumsiest dancer in the world would improve by dancing with him. We had danced one round of the old Carolingian pavane and were just beginning the second when suddenly Ronsard stopped. "Your Majesty?" His voice was filled with alarm. At that moment I felt as if my face had — it sounds so strange — floated away from my head. It was indeed a disembodied thing. "Milady, your face!" The next thing I knew I was on the floor. People were bending over me saying the strangest things.

"It has swollen to the size of a melon!"

"She is as red as a strawberry!"

"Look, her eyes are locked." And indeed it did feel as if my eyes had frozen in their sockets, for I could not blink. A footman carried me to my chambers and the King's physician was called, as was Ruggieri. It was not long before I heard the word I dreaded. "Leeches."

"No! No! No!" I screamed. Janet Sinclair rushed to my side to calm me. As much as I love Janet, I really wanted my mother.

"You must have them, my dear. You have had a bad reaction to the face whitening. It can happen sometimes. The leeches must be brought to suck out the poison."

Just then the royal apothecary arrived with two immense jars, the insides of which were a writhing slime of black leeches. I could not even shut my eyes for my eyelids were still frozen open. With long tweezers Ruggieri and the King's doctor, de la Romaniére, placed the leeches one by one on my face and neck and chest. My face being numb I could not exactly feel them sucking but I fancy that I heard them. I thought I would go mad. I wished my own doctor, Doctor Bourgoing, were here, but he is gone temporarily. He would never have put leeches on me. All night my face remained under this blanket of leeches. I somehow managed to sleep with my eyes open because they had dosed me with a strong spirit. By morning I was really no better, but I saw thin threads of blood trickling down my chest where the leeches had gorged and been pulled from my skin.

Suddenly Nostradamus burst into the room with Lord Erskine at his side. "Get those foul things off her!" he roared. He came to my bedside and began pulling off the leeches. Next he dipped a sponge into a bowl that Lord Erskine held. He began wiping my face. There was a strong scent of cloves. Then with his fingertips he began massaging my face. He called for "ointment of calamus," which he next put on thickly, and then he folded a hot wet cloth, also soaked in the same palm-scented lotion, and placed it on my face. Gradually the numbness began to leave. He applied more lotions and ointments.

Then little Mary Fleming with tears streaming down her face cried out, "Mary, you are back!"

I tried pressing my lips together and then making a slight smile. They felt normal. "Might I see a mirror?" I asked. Lord Erskine brought me a mirror. I looked at my reflection. Never have I been so happy to see that band of freckles across my nose. I looked deathly pale with blue shadows under my eyes, but my face was my face once more.

Nostradamus sank into a chair. "A toxic beauty they all strive for."

I turned my head to him. "You mean the whitening."

"Precisely, my dear. You were lucky. You found out quickly how poisonous it was to you. But the ceruse made of vinegar and white lead builds up over years and years until finally a woman dies from her own reserve of poison slowly administered over a lifetime of seeking beauty. Her fingernails turn blue. She loses feeling in her fingertips and toes and earlobes, but she is beset by the sensation of fiery ants eating into her skull. Finally the poison creeps into the muscles of the throat and paralyzes them. She cannot swallow to eat and then soon she cannot breathe."

What a terrible, terrible death I have been spared. I shall forbid the four Marys ever to use the whitening again. I know I am lucky, but still to be so sick and so far away from my mother leaves me with another kind of pain that is so deep.

FEBRURY 11, 1554

I've managed to be excused from many ballet practices. It was almost worth having leeches on my face. But I think I would endure leeches again if I could have my mother with me, my mother's hand in mine.

FEBRUARY 12, 1554

How shall I ever thank Doctor Nostradamus? I cannot think of a way. The four Marys came to visit me today, and so did Francis. I am allowed to play only quiet games.

Francis and I were playing chess, and he said the strangest things as we moved our pieces on the board. He said that his mother and father are talking about an alliance between France and Spain and are looking to the Duke of Castille for either Princess Elizabeth or Princess Claude. Francis picked up a pawn and said to me, "Did it ever strike you, Mary, that we are not so much children and sons and daughters of parents as we are pieces on a gigantic chessboard called Europe? You are given to me to help checkmate England."

Francis's words struck me so deeply that I picked up a pawn and looked at it. Thinking aloud, I whispered softly, "But I am a Queen."

Then Francis said, "And I am the Dauphin and what does it all mean?"

FEBRUARY 13, 1554

I am feeling much better, but everyone insists that I stay abed. This is so vexing, because the weather is fine, the sun shines, and the four Marys and Francis go out hawking and riding every day. Little Princess Claude comes to visit and reads to me, as my eyes are still not quite right. But my eyes would be fine for riding. I am terribly bored.

February 15, 1554

We are leaving for Chenonceau. My timing is good. I recovered just in time to go on the last hunt and yet miss the last ballet practice. It has turned very cold.

February 17, 1554

"The river is frozen!" Mary Beaton cried, leaning out from our carriage as we drove up to the château. Chenonceau spans the river Cher. It rises from the water. Indeed the oldest part of the château was originally a water mill. But much has been done to it. King Henry gave it as a gift to Diane de Poitiers many years ago, and she has made it even more beautiful. But the part that we children love the most is the bridge that connects the château to the opposite side of the riverbank. When the river is frozen, it is so much fun to skate under the bridge and in and around the pilings. We play tag and hide-and-seek on skates. But one must be very careful near the stone pilings for oftentimes the ice is not solid there and one could fall through.

Naturally our plans for skating were squashed because Queen Catherine insists on one last practice of the ballet, which we are to give tonight. But then, thank heavens, we shall be done with this fool thing.

Madame de Parois has received a diagnosis of dropsy, an affliction that causes one to swell up. Mary Fleming dared a peek at her legs. She pretended to drop something under the card table when we were playing, and she said Madame de Parois had her stockings rolled down and her dress hitched up and that her legs looked like tree trunks. No ankles to speak of. Now I feel very bad for her. I have sought out Father Confessor and have told him of my regret in thinking such — well, not evil, but unkind — thoughts about Madame de Parois. I cannot make formal confession for I have not yet made my First Communion. Father Mamerot and my uncle the Cardinal will decide when that will happen. I am anxious, of course, but I know I am not ready. For in truth, in regard to Madame de Parois, I ask myself, If her legs went back to normal, if she did not have the dropsy, would I really try to improve my behavior? Probably not. I therefore do not think I am ready for my First Communion. The woman does vex me so, fat legs or not. I wish I had more patience with her. I wish I could ignore her often beastly ways. But I can't. I suppose this is a character flaw within me. I have discussed all this with Father Confessor. I am not sure if saying a thousand rosaries would help me. In any case, Doctor de la Romaniére, the King's physician, has sent her to Paris. She will be more comfortable there, and she has a sister who can help care for her.

FEBRUARY 19, 1554

The ballet is over. I did quite well for missing so many practices when I was sick. Diane de Poitiers clapped loudly. The Queen looked quite pleased. She had made up many of the steps and the King was very enthusiastic, clapping harder than anyone else. His sister Marguerite de Valois was also in attendance, and she and the King both praised Queen Catherine. I must say the Queen did seem to shine and was as close as she can ever get to beauty and resplendence. There is a rumor that she is expecting again. She is always most happy when she is with child. That is why I suppose she is with child so often — at least seven times since I have come to live here — once with twins but they died as infants. I think it is the one thing that she knows she can do for the King that Diane cannot. Diane is too old to have babies, but she is not too old to be beautiful. But the King paid most attention to the Queen. I think that is how it should be, even though I don't like the Queen very much. In public I believe he should pay the most attention to the Queen. The four Marys and I discuss this endlessly.

FEBRUARY 20, 1554

Skating today. Lovely ice. Of course twenty footmen and another dozen or so servants had been scraping it and making it perfect for us children. Even with perfect ice Francis had a terrible time. He is so awkward on anything but a horse. The blacksmith from the stables made some tiny blades for the shoes of little Henry and Charles. Mary Seton and I skate around with the babes between our legs. The little boys are quite wobbly. I think it will be awhile before they are sturdy enough to skate on their own. Puff enjoys the ice very much. She skitters about and then has this trick of skidding on her belly. Thimble is simply too little to bring out in this cold.

I have been on my knees praying all night. A terrible thing has occurred. Mary Beaton, so strong and bold, might be dying. Here is what happened. We were skating today. Mary Seton and I had the babies between our legs when all of a sudden Puff skidded on her belly across the ice toward one of the bridge pilings where the ice was much thinner. The dog broke through. We heard her desperate barks. Mary Beaton was the closest, without thinking and really just full of good heart, she skated toward the little dog. Before she was even close, the ice cracked and she went under. We all started screaming. We saw Mary surface and grasp for a hold, but the ice broke off. None of us knows how to swim, and if we could it would be impossible with our hoops and kirtles and chemises and cloaks. The guards came with long poles and ropes. They tied the ropes to Robin MacClean, my head guardsman. He and another man crept out across the ice. They did break through, but being on tethers they did not go under. We were all screaming, "Mary! Mary!"

"I can't find anything," Robin yelled back. And then very courageously he dove under the ice! He seemed gone for the longest time. When he surfaced he had not Mary but Puff. But where was Mary?

"Tie me! Tie me!" I yelled at another guard. "I must go and find my Mary."

Then a minute later Robin shouted. "I have her!" Somehow he attached a rope around her waist, and they dragged her up. But her body seemed to be lifeless as Robin MacClean staggered ashore with her in his arms. Her skin was blue and her eyes half shut and I could see only the whites. Someone in the meantime had taken Puff and cried out, "The pup lives." But in that moment I cared not about Puff at all. I was glad Puff was alive, but I did not know whether my dear Mary Beaton would survive the night.

Nor do I yet. She is unconscious, her breathing ragged. A priest has been called for Last Rites. All I can think is that Mary must not die. How can God save a lapdog and not Mary? I shall not leave Mary's bedside. I shall keep a vigil all night long.

FEBRUARY 22, 1554

The sky has grown dark. The stars break out. And still Mary is unconscious.

February 23, 1554

Another day and night passes. I cannot stand the yapping of the dogs. I try not to hate Puff.

Later

Dawn creeps in to chase out the night. But no pink tints my Mary's cheeks. Her breathing is hoarse like the north wind that rasps on the copper sheathing of the roof's edge. Diane de Poitiers comes to sit with me. She is the only one I shall allow. The other Marys beg to come, but I will not let them. It is too harsh a sight. Robust Mary has grown old before my eyes. Her eyes seem to sink into her head; her skin draws tight over her cheekbones. She already looks skeletal, her head like a skull. Diane holds my hand.

Later still

How to describe this moment? I had been asleep in the chair by Mary Beaton's bed. Suddenly I felt a myriad of sensations, a feeling of warmth, then a draft, and the sense of a strange presence. I felt first a blade of sunlight fall from a high window and strike my cheek. Then something stirred. My first thought: Was it the spirit of Mary crossing over? But then no. A voice, older than time, creaky as a hinge. "Milady."

"Mary!" Diane gasped. "Mary! She wakes!"

I was suddenly alert. I looked at Mary Beaton. Her eyes were open. Her face flushed. "What has happened?"

"Oh, Mary!" Diane and I both cried and grasped her hands. "Oh, Mary, you're back."

"Let me get the other Marys," Diane said, jumping up.

"Oh, yes, do fetch them. Quick!" I cried.

FEBRUARY 24, 1554

We are so joyous with the return of our Mary Beaton. Mary tells me I must not blame Puff and I guess I don't, but something has changed in my feelings for the little dog, I am sorry to admit. I think Mary Beaton senses this and in some way so does Puff. She seems to pull toward Mary Beaton like a heavenly sphere toward a sun, just the way Lord Erskine described the theories of Copernicus and his belief of how the planets circle the sun.

FEBRUARY 25, 1554

The river has melted, and I am not at all sad to see the ice go, after all that has happened. Indeed almost overnight it seems as if spring is upon us. The four Marys and I sat in my smaller dining salon at the round table that sits in the curve of the tower, and looked out upon the greening fields beyond the river. We sipped our steaming chocolate and ate the flaky brioche buns with jam. The sunlight streamed in, and it was as if we were caught in a web of golden light. In that moment I realized how fragile life is, and in knowing its frailty it had become all the more precious.

It will take Mary awhile to get her strength back. The court is to go to Paris soon, but I am to go first to Meudon, the de Guise château, to visit my mother's family. Uncle Francis and Aunt Anne's new babe should be born soon, and there will be a christening. And I shall also visit my grandmother Antoinette, whom I have not seen for many months.

FEBRUARY 27, 1554

The days pass quietly, as none of us Marys want to leave Mary Beaton for a second. So we curtail our outdoor activities. Queen Catherine speaks about another ballet.

Lord spare us! However, she spends much time with Ruggieri in his tower, peering into mirrors and crystal balls. You see, Nostradamus has gone back to his home in Salon to the south, where he has a wife and children. We hear that Doctor Nostradamus has very much a mind of his own. He is no sycophant, no self-seeking oily flatterer like Ruggieri. He has told the Queen that he will come to Paris only on certain occasions, but that he must be with his family. We hear that she offered to move his family into luxurious quarters in the Louvre Palace in Paris, but he said no. Nonetheless the Queen needs her seers, especially during her pregnancies, so she relies on Ruggieri in Nostradamus's absence. I do not understand this. If the seer tells her what will happen, that a child might die in infancy or that she might miscarry and it is fate, what good does it do to know about it in advance? It is my view that such tellers of the future and seers kill hope, and without hope it is nearly impossible to live. Hope is the air that our spirits breathe. Without it our spirits suffocate. Could I go on if I were to know that I may never see my mother again? No, I do not think I could. But I live each day in hope of seeing dear Mother and my birth land again.

February 28, 1554

We found out today that the rumor of Queen Catherine's pregnancy was not true. Indeed I do believe that she thought she was expecting for a time, for she did seem to glow and now she seems her same grim self. However, I have no doubt that she will soon be with child.

March 1, 1554

The meadows turn a soft green and dissolve into the deeper green of the forest. The swans come out of their winter roosts and sail the river Cher like small galleons. I see a faint lavender mist hovering over a field. It is the thyme about to bloom. I am mightily distracted by these signs and emblems of spring. My Latin master, George Buchanan, frets over my careless translations. My mathematics tutor cannot believe that my mind goes blank when I try to add fractions. Ronsard spoke sharply to me as he explained the complicated meter of an ancient Greek poem. It is Ronsard who jolts me from my reveries. "They say your British cousin Elizabeth, daughter of Henry VIII, is a formidable scholar."

I blink. "Is she not imprisoned now by her sister, Queen Mary of England?"

"Yes indeed. But there is talk that the Queen suffers and might soon die. And the people love Princess Elizabeth."

"Do you think that Queen Mary might harm her?"

"I sincerely hope not. For Elizabeth has a wisdom and wit that befits a Queen."

I immediately settle down to the business of this ancient Greek poem.

MARCH 2, 1554

Father Mamerot has sought me out. He has asked that I examine my conscience in regard to Queen Catherine. He questions me so gently that indeed it makes me feel worse. Perhaps I would do better with one of those harsh confessors who immediately assigns severe penance. But that is not Father Mamerot's way. He asks that I go deeper. He wonders, Is it pride that makes me behave in a manner that is often rude to Queen Catherine. Is it envy? Never. Perhaps it is pride. I am not sure. I just do not care for her. I must reflect on all this, he told me. I looked up questioningly. He read my mind: "I shall give you no penance because, Mary, until you understand why you do what you do, your rosaries shall not be heard by God."

MARCH 3, 1554

Mary Beaton is well enough to travel, so the court moves on to Paris, but I wait here for a few days before going to Meudon. I miss the Marys but Diane is here still, and she promises that we shall take a long riding journey through Touraine and spend the night at the convent of the Calvarian sisters and at the abbey of Fontevrault. I look forward to this with great excitement. It shall be just Diane and myself and of course our guards. My Scots guardsmen, however, shall exchange what they are wearing for the simple clothes of French horse grooms and equerries of noble houses. And after this tour I shall go on to Meudon to see Grandmama and my uncles and new baby cousin.

P.S. I have tried to think about what Father Mamerot has said. But as soon as I try to think about it, other things creep into my mind. It seems so slippery. In one instant I can think: Oh, yes, I shall be much nicer to Queen Catherine, but then I think of her directing us in that ballet. So sure of herself. She is the proud one. And it is not just the ballet. It is the way she encourages her courtiers to fawn about her. The way she declares herself to be the authority, the final word on everything from fashion to food to sculpture to perfume, for goodness sakes.

This has been so exciting. Diane and I have traveled in disguise with none of the royal standards or emblems. Yes, we have our guards, but to people in the villages and the countryside, we just appear as French noblewomen out for a day's ride. They do not know how far we go — perhaps to visit relatives in a nearby château — for we travel light. Our *porte-bagages* without clothes can easily be carried on the backs of horses. Here at the Inn of the Two Ducks, which indeed is by a pond with many more than two ducks, we ate the simple fare of country folk: a thick, hearty soup that tasted wonderful after the chill of riding all day, crusty bread, and sausage cut in thick slices. The sausage was the best and I commented to Diane. She said the country folk are very thrifty and use nearly every part of the pig. And then she said the most amusing thing I think I have ever heard. She said that after they have made all their hams and sausages, there is nothing left of the pig but the squeal.

LATER

Diane and I share a bed at the inn. She still sleeps, but it is just dawn, and if I sit here by the window with a taper lit, there is enough light for me to write. Diane and I whispered into the night. I mentioned to her about the new ballet that Queen Catherine wants us to perform in the summer at Château Amboise. "How lovely!" Diane said, and I said I did not think it was at all lovely.

And then it just slipped out of me, a question I have long pondered. "Diane, how can you be so nice to the Queen when you are the one who really loves the King and when she, as she so often does, treats you with scorn?"

Diane said, "Yes, she sometimes treats me with scorn, but she also listens to me — about you children, about the court, about the King's advisers — for she knows that the King really loves me." Then she sighed and said, "The poor thing — *la pauvre.*"

"I cannot believe that you feel sorry for her," I said.

"To be unloved is not easy."

"Her children love her." But it went unspoken that they love Diane more.

Diane then said something very mysterious to me. "You must learn love through being loved."

"Was Queen Catherine never loved?"

"Both her parents died when she was an infant, not even a month old. She was a cradle orphan. She grew up in terrible danger, for although she was the Duchess of Florence, the Florentines rose up in civil war against the Medicis and assaulted their palace. As a child of eight she was caught in a revolution. They had to take her to a monastery for safety."

I thought of my own past. Of the great Battle of Pinkie Cleugh and how indeed I had been taken to the monastery of Inchmahome. But I was with my mother and my four Marys. There was always someone nearby who I knew loved me dearly.

"Did she have any friends?" I asked, thinking of the four Marys.

"No. I think not. I think Queen Catherine has never had any friends."

That is sad. I must find it in my heart to try harder with this difficult woman.

Yesterday after leaving the Inn of the Two Ducks we rode here to the Abbey of Fontevrault. We arrived in the evening. We spent the night in what is called the Grand Moustier, which is the convent for the nuns. This is a strange place. One feels the presence of many ghosts — the ghosts of lepers and victims of the most horrible and disfiguring diseases — for once there was a hospital. Also the ghosts of penitent women as well as the ghosts of those women battered and beaten by their husbands or fathers who sought refuge with the nuns. And the ghosts of the Plantagenets, the royal French family of Anjou from which came some of England's and France's most illustrious Kings and Queens. Diane and I wandered through the deep shadows of the chapel where the Plantagenets lie in their eternal sleep. We found the tombs of King Henry II, King of both England and France four hundred years ago, and his wife, Eleanor of Aquitaine. She is a heroine of both Diane de Poitier's and mine. Daring and bold she traveled all the way to Turkey and Palestine on the Second Crusade.

And then there was the tomb of their son Richard the Lionhearted, who became King of England and also went to the Holy Land to fight. So I walked amongst these ghosts. And suddenly I had a thought. Suppose I had lived four hundred years ago and by some strange quirk of fate had been sent to the court of Eleanor of Aquitaine to be married to her son Richard. Would I have liked her any better or any less than I do Queen Catherine? She is said to have been very strong willed. I think perhaps no kingdom can have two Queens, even if the Queens be kind and loving or pliable and retiring.

Tomorrow we go to Chinon and the citadel where Joan of Arc stayed.

March 6, 1554
Convent of the Calvarian Sisters, Chinon

I cannot believe that I ride the same streets that Joan of Arc rode a little more than a hundred years ago. She defended her country and saw that the rightful King was crowned, but then she was captured, called a witch, tried, and burned at the stake. How did she have the courage?

She was a peasant girl who knew not how to read or write, and yet they say she died with grace. How does one learn that?

Diane and I are silent as we ride through Chinon. Our heads swirl with many thoughts and there is something unspeakable about all we think. Here is one thought that I cannot utter but I may write. Had Joan of Arc not been a woman who dared to dress as a man would they have called that person a witch or merely a traitor? Perhaps it does not matter. Either way the person would have died.

MARCH 7, 1554

We have passed two days here in this peaceful convent. I have had much time to reflect. I have not examined my conscience in regard to Queen Catherine as directed by Father Mamerot as much as perhaps I should have. Instead my head is filled with thoughts of Joan of Arc. Her life, her vision. You know that she was finally found innocent of all of which she had been condemned. There is a book here at the convent that Diane showed me. It contains a letter from Joan of Arc's mother, an official request to the Pope, many years after her daughter was burned, to recognize her daughter's innocence. Tears sprang to my eyes as I read it. Her letter begins "I had a daughter," and then she proceeds to tell what a good and devout child her Joan was, and then speaks of her enemies. The trial was indeed finally declared "tainted with fraud," and Joan of Arc was in death pronounced innocent. But I do not think I have ever read any sadder words than those four of Joan's mother, Isabelle of Arc, "I had a daughter . . ." God forbid I should ever say those words.

MARCH 8, 1554
CHÂTEAU MEUDON, NEAR PARIS

It is wonderful to see Grandmama again. She seems much the same. Although she is of vast age, she never seems any older, not from when I first met her when I came to France six years ago. But I know that she has more than six decades. Her hands are densely wrinkled like crêpe silk. The skin is so thin that the veins show through dark and purple, and they bump up. She always teases me when I come, for she remembers that as a young child I asked her in my very babylike French, "Madame, pourquoi vos mains sont commes les griffes d'un poulet? (Madame, why are your hands like chicken claws?)" I can hardly imagine that I said that. But I must have, for ever since, Grandmama pulls off her net gloves after kissing me, gives a little chicken cackle, and asks if I want to see her hands. Her eyes are faded and rheumy and I can tell that she has stiffness in her back, but even with all this and her chicken-claw hands there is something young about Grandmama. I think it is her humor, her readiness to laugh. I do not think in truth I have ever heard Catherine de Medici laugh. When I come here, I always know there will be many occasions for laughter. Grandmama can make even my uncles laugh, and they are the most serious men I know.

We do have this time some serious business at Meudon. Now I must finally sign the papers for my mother to become Queen Regent. There is also some unpleasant business to attend to concerning Lord Arran, the Duke of Châtelherault. But first Grandmama wants to show me the improvements made to Meudon.

MARCH 9, 1554

I am very tired. This was not an easy day. I, of course, had to sign the papers that make my mother Queen Regent, but there was the unpleasantness with Lord Arran. It has been discovered that Lord Arran, who was in charge of the treasury, the jewels, and the plate of the estates of Scotland, had been guilty of "defalcations," which means stealing from the treasury when one is a guardian of that treasury. So first I signed the papers, and then Lord Arran was called in to the grand gallery. I sat in a special chair, the Chair of Estate with the emblems of both my father's family, the Royal House of Stuart, and my mother's, the de Guise family, the House of Lorraine. Over the Chair of Estate is the royal canopy. I had rehearsed with my uncles and my grandmama what I was to say. (And to think I had once worried about signing my name and dribbling ink! This was much harder.) But I spoke it well and in a strong voice. "Lord Arran, Duke of Châtelherault, as Queen of the Scots and instrument of the Queen Regent, my mother, I inform you that you are as of this day, this hour, and this minute discharged of your official duties as Lord Governor of the Estates of Scotland and ordered to make restitution to the estates, treasury of the jewels, and plate that you have taken without authority or permission. You are found by the Crown liable and responsible. The Queen Regent in her infinite mercy and the King of France, my own representative in this country, allow that you may keep your titles, but repayment with interest is demanded. Do you accept these requirements?"

"I do, Your Majesty."

"Go thee to thy confessor and make your peace with our Lord Jesus Christ, our Savior, now that you have made peace with your Queen."

This was my first royal act. I wish it had not been a "scolding." I would have liked to have done something grand and wonderful, something that would improve the lot of a nation and not merely reprimand one greedy soul.

I had received from my dear mother a letter counseling me on Lord Arran. This was one that I was not supposed to show to my uncle. So she provided another to show him. It seems my mother feels that there are some treacherous people in the court who might try to intervene and plot on the Lord's behalf. She cautions me to be aware. As she always does in her letters, she concludes with the words concerning how a sovereign must always proceed with caution and circumspection, and never on sheer impulse.

MARCH 10, 1554

I have written a letter to Mother about the signing of the papers making her the Queen Regent. I sent her my best tidings and told her of my meeting with Lord Arran. I did not want to boast, so I said only that I spoke in a strong, unwavering voice and that Lord Arran accepted our charges with grace and that I then commended him to seek his Father Confessor. I am sure that will please Mother. I told her that we are expecting the birth of a new little cousin any moment and that King Henry and Queen Catherine are intending to come for the christening.

LATER

Aunt Anne has begun her lying in. Grandmama therefore cannot go to the grotto with me, as she must attend the birth. I am not allowed. This is most boring for me. I spend my time trying to teach Thimble a trick — jumping through a hoop. He learns it too quickly. What should I teach him next? A Greek poem?

MARCH 11, 1554

Aunt Anne still labors!

LATER

Still no baby.

MIDNIGHT

A baby boy! He is most adorable. Grandmama came to fetch me. He is plump with cheeks like the rosiest Normandy apples, and he has lots of black hair that sticks straight out from his head. The christening will be in a few days. I hope Francis comes. It seems like forever since I last saw him, and I do miss my Marys but I know they will not be coming.

MARCH 16, 1554

The baby was christened this morning. His name is Charles, and he shall be given the title the Duke of Mayenne. I was permitted a place of honor in the chapel and stood next to my uncle the Cardinal to hold the babe's cap when it was removed for the Cardinal to sprinkle on the holy water.

I am feeling a bit poorly now, as I think I ate too much at the luncheon. My grandmama's table is renowned. At least four kinds of birds were served — swan, peacock, capons, and my favorite, heron. There were artichokes and chestnuts cooked with white asparagus. And so many different tarts — plum, apple, custard.

I am trying to improve my manner with the Queen. Would you believe that I even inquired about our ballet master Balthazar? Would one ever imagine that I would dare bring up the subject of ballet? I think even Queen Catherine was surprised. I inquired not only about the ballet master but also Madame de Parois. I *am* trying. It seems to me that there should be something the opposite of confession. One should be able to go and tell of one's small moral triumphs. But I suppose that would make one guilty of pride — yet another sin to confess. A vicious circle, I suppose.

MARCH 17, 1554

I am so furious with Queen Catherine. I cannot believe what that horrible, insensitive woman did at the banquet table this evening. She sent her *valet de chambre* over to tell Francis to blow his nose more often, "for the good of his health." Well, it is not for the good of his health to be so corrected in public. That woman has the sensitivity of a wild boar. And she looks like one, too. Poor Francis was mortified. I wished so hard in that instant that my nose would start to run. I would never have wiped it. I would have let it just dribble onto the roasted duck, right over the asparagus, maybe onto the little potatoes, and then I would like to be seized by a huge sneeze and spray all over that Italian merchant's daughter and blow her right back to Italy. I don't care if she was orphaned when she was two weeks old. She spent much time with the nuns in a convent. She should have learned some tenderness.

P.S. I must say that writing something as I just did really makes me feel ever so much better than confession would. I suppose, however, that I shall have to seek out Father Confessor Mamerot when I return with the royal family to Paris and the Louvre Palace tomorrow. It is the beginning of Holy Week. We are always in Paris to celebrate Easter.

MARCH 18, 1554
LE LOUVRE PALACE, PARIS

It is so hard to be in Paris as spring begins. It is really not the place to be. Thank heaven the four Marys are here. We may all complain together. Spring in the French countryside is magical. We should be at Chambord, or Chenonceau, or Anet, or Fontainebleau, but not here in this smelly old city. The palace is near the marketplace, and we smell all the awful smells — blood from the meat market and the old rotten vegetables that they keep too long, then throw into garbage heaps in the farmers' market. And then the street gutters swirl with swill — swill I will not describe, for it would be most indelicate. But you might imagine, for much of Paris does not have proper privies.

MARCH 19, 1554

A letter from Mother and a small package as well. In the package was a paper carefully folded, and when I unfolded it a handkerchief fell out with a scattering of dried petals — petals of heather and harebells, thistle and gorse. It was as if all the Highlands of Scotland had flooded into my room. Just at that moment Janet Sinclair entered. Her eyes widened in great amazement. She looked about as if to catch the wafting breeze of some spirit or sprite that had suddenly stirred the air. Because indeed it felt as if some presence had entered the room. "What is it?" she asked, her eyes darting about my chamber as if to catch a glimpse of this illusive spirit.

"It is this," I said, and I gathered the petals into the handkerchief and held it out to her. "My mother sent it with the letter I received from her this day."

She took the handkerchief from me and pressed it to her nose, all the while mumbling softly in Gaelic, *"Michty aye . . . michty aye,* yes, yes . . . *Chuffed . . ."* "Pleased," "delighted," and *doss,* "magic" . . . her words spilled out.

Janet speaks a Gaelic different from mine, so although the words are often similar I do not always understand her. No matter, it was all very Scots. All words to describe that dear rough country from whence we came. She tells me about that land with its craggy headlands and outcroppings, its fields of green stippled with bright yellow gorse, rocky ledges to which the most delicate flowers somehow cling and find a niche to grow. Scotland!

Janet had come in to discuss with me what I would be wearing to the Services of the Shadows, those held in the evening on the Wednesday before Easter. I really loathe the Wednesday service that we all go to at Saint Denis. Queen Catherine insists that we all wear our most dark and somber clothes. The services are after dark in the cathedral of Saint Denis where many of the French Kings and Queens are buried. After the passage from Matthew is read that describes how one man offered a sponge dipped in vinegar to Christ while he was on the cross, the priest passes through with a cloth soaked in vinegar for us to touch our lips to. We never did this in Scotland. I think it is something that came from Italy with Queen Catherine.

Her uncle was, after all, a Pope. But I don't like it, and it's not just the sting of the vinegar.

MARCH 21, 1554

Thank heavens the Service of the Shadows is behind me. I am not going back to Saint Denis until Easter Sunday. I am going to pretend that I am sick. I have had some stomach complaints of late and all I have to do is tell Doctor Bourgoing. Doctor Bourgoing is very young and nice, and he might even suspect that I am pretending, for I have done this before when I want to avoid certain occasions, especially those in which Queen Catherine dominates. That cathedral gives me the shivers. I do not know why but here in France they have what I can only describe as a dark practice in the burial of royalty. They cut out the heart of the dead King or Queen or Dauphin. They then embalm the rest of the body and put the heart in a vial filled with strong preservative fluids and place it in the reliquary of the cathedral. I think it is awful being dismembered in such a manner. The idea of going to one's grave with parts missing is very disturbing to me. I must take this up with my uncles. I do not want this done to me. If I am Queen of Scotland and someday am to be Queen of

France, I think as the ruler of two realms I should get to choose how I want to be dealt with after death. If the French object I am just going to say "Bury me in Scotland." I do remember that still and misty graveyard on the island of Inchmahome in the middle of Lake Mentieth where I was taken after the Battle of Pinkie Cleugh.

When we went to the cathedral for the Service of the Shadows, I took the handkerchief my mother had sent me. The fragrance was still strong, and when they passed the cloth soaked in vinegar, I barely put it to my lips and just afterward pressed the handkerchief to my nose. I closed my eyes and for a few brief seconds I was in a place of no shadows, no dark priest with vinegar cloths, no Kings without hearts. Scotland filled my mind and for a few fleeting seconds I was home.

MARCH 24, 1554

Wonderful news. Lord Erskine tells me that a new music teacher has been hired to replace Monsieur Boulon, who has been ailing all these months. He is to join us at Fontainebleau, for which we leave right after Easter. I must practice my lute and I would practice the cithara, but I think it is out of tune, and its strings are nearly impossible to tune unless one is an expert. I hope this new teacher, Signore Marcellini, will be able to do it. I do want to ask Lord Erskine about the possibility of having some Scottish musicians sent here to court. Now that I have my own household, I think that we should have the music of Scotland. I would like at least half a dozen bagpipers. The music of the pipes always puts me in the best of humors; I think it balances them. Indeed, I have talked with Doctor Bourgoing about this theory of music and the correct balance of humors. I like Doctor Bourgoing, for he always takes time to explain. Anyhow I think he agrees with me about the humors and the beneficial effects of music.

There are four humors — blood, black bile, phlegm, and yellow bile. These four humors originate in the heart, spleen, brain, and liver. An imbalance can cause a person to be hopeful, or sad, or listless, or quick to anger. I think that I am nicely balanced. Poor Francis, however, shows every sign of an excess of phlegm, thus making him listless, and his mother, Queen Catherine, undoubtedly has a surfeit of yellow bile. She is a bilious person and so quick to anger. The most perfectly balanced person I know is Diane de Poitiers. And I would say the second most perfectly balanced is Mary Beaton. However, I think music would help us all — especially the music of the bag-pipers. I would be happy to let them play for Queen Catherine.

MARCH 26, 1554

I am so excited. This evening there was a small concert held in the grand salon and after the performance I was standing talking with Francis, Mary Seton, and Mary Livingston. René the Florentine, one of the perfumers Queen Catherine brought with her from Italy — and who, I might add, is much more agreeable than Ruggieri and many others she brought along — turned toward us and sniffed the air. "I smell an essence most delectable. Is it campanula and . . ."

"Harebells, Sir. My mother sent me a handkerchief. Here, I keep it knotted in my sleeve." I withdrew the hand-kerchief and carefully untied it. The dried bit of heather and harebells and gorse were revealed.

The signore bent over my hand. He has very large nos-trils — cavernous nostrils. I was afraid that he might in-hale all the bits. But he didn't. "Your Majesty," he said, "let me ask the next courier who goes to Scotland to bring back some of these petals. I shall send proper packing materials so they will arrive fresh. Then let me try to brew an *absolue*, an essence from them, and therefore you can always keep fresh that memory of Scotland." He looked now directly into my eyes.

"How kind," I said. "I would love that."

I held the handkerchief to my nose and breathed in the now faint scent. Each day it has faded away a bit more. How wonderful to have forever a bottle of this scent if indeed René the Florentine could achieve it. What is it about the way a scent works on one's mind? It erases the boundaries of time and place. I remember just recently at Grandmama's smelling the calvados brandy she poured for my uncles, and suddenly I was back in Normandy at Château Saint-Germain. I sniffed at the handkerchief once more. There can, however, be something about a scent that bruises the heart. I think of my mother, and the sharpness of missing her is as fresh as on the day when she left France after her visit nearly three years ago.

MARCH 31, 1554
CHÂTEAU FONTAINEBLEAU

Madame de Parois has rejoined us and is as cranky as ever.

I am to have my portrait painted by Clouet. My mother has requested the painting, and although Niccolo dell'Abate has great talent, he is considered much too fanciful for my mother's or my grandmother's taste. He poses his subjects in mythological landscapes. Mother wants a full-length portrait of me in front of my Chair of Estate with the Scottish symbols as well as those of the House of Lorraine. I am to wear a dress that my uncles are bringing that was specially made for the portrait. They come tomorrow.

APRIL 1, 1554

The dress that my grandmother sent is of a deadly weight! I do not know how anyone could ever be expected to wear it to a ball. The bodice stiff with jewels must weigh as much as a knight's armor. I tired after a quarter of an hour of posing. To make matters worse, it has turned unseasonably hot. So all the other children and the four Marys are out playing near the grand fountain for which this château is named. This fountain rises in five great spouts from a natural rock formation, and it is the perfect place to picnic on a hot day. How I would love to be there. Instead I stand in Clouet's studio here at Fontainebleau in this horrid dress, being tortured. I think I would indeed prefer to stand naked for this portrait than wear this infernal dress. It is not hard to have a solemn look on one's face. However, Clouet tells me that my look turns sour. I must not appear a sour Queen. Queen Mary of England apparently is a very sour-looking queen, he tells me.

LATER

Another session with Clouet. Clouet has much information. I asked him about Queen Mary, who is my cousin. He told me that she has what he describes as a "peculiar" personality. I pressed him. So he told me that she never really forgave her father for divorcing her mother, Catherine of Aragon, and marrying Anne Boleyn. She believes Anne Boleyn was a witch and believes that the daughter of Anne Boleyn and Henry VIII, Princess Elizabeth, my cousin and her half-sister, is a bastard child, and that Mary has imprisoned her! But that is not all. Queen Mary orders Protestants burned to death and anyone else who does not believe in the sacraments of the Catholic Church. I believe fervently in the sacraments of the Catholic Church, and so I despair of this rebel John Knox, who leads the Scottish Reformation and its attempts to rid Scotland of the Catholic Church. But would I burn the man and any others who did not believe in my faith and the sacraments? I think not. No! Most certainly. I not only think not. I know never!

Our discussions during my posing help pass the time. The weight of this jeweled bodice seems light compared with the weight that rests on a crowned head. Someday I shall be called upon to lead my country, and what shall I do with these reformers?

APRIL 9, 1554

Tonight I stand in front of my mirror half naked. The skin on my midriff is blotchy and red with the imprints from the jeweled bodice in which I posed again today. Clouet tells me that once he has the bodice painted I can exchange the dress for something more comfortable. I am perhaps growing accustomed to the weight and the press of this dress. Or perhaps it is that I am mightily distracted by our conversations. I think constantly of this Queen Mary, my cousin. They do indeed call her Bloody Mary. How terrible to be written down in the pages of history with such a name. And when I do not think of her, I think of the imprisoned Princess Elizabeth. Clouet says she is quite beautiful and greatly resembles me with her red hair. Am I prettier? I dare not ask, for that would make me seem vain. But how does this beautiful princess pass her days? She is nearly ten years older than I am, yet I feel a bond. How I would like to meet her someday. I said in the session this morning to Clouet, for I was idly dreaming as he painted me, that perhaps I will write her a letter since we are cousins. I was startled from my dreams by the clatter of a paintbrush. Yes, Clouet dropped his paintbrush to the floor. His eyes opened wide with terror. "Your Majesty, that would be most unwise. Supposing word came of this to Queen Mary? She would immediately suspect a plot against her."

Of course he is right. How could I be so ignorant? How could I make such a blunder? With the stroke of my pen I could upset the delicate relationship between France and England. I could jeopardize my mother in Scotland. I could jeopardize all my Scots subjects. I am mortified by my own stupidity. My eyes welled with tears. The posing session was halted and I was excused. Now I stand here bare in my stupidity before my mirror, the impression of the jeweled bodice still upon my skin. Will I ever truly be fit to be the Queen I have already been crowned? I must temper my feelings, hold my tongue, and be less impulsive and more considered in my thoughts. I must grow up. I resolve to do this.

April 15, 1554

Perhaps it is a sign, but my uncle the Cardinal came to me today and informed me that I am to begin preparations for my First Communion. What better indication could I have that it is time for me to grow up? Am I ready? I am not sure. Have I sufficiently reflected and examined my conscience? Many things in life have come easily to me. I am skillful with my hawks in the field. I ride expertly. I was quick to master the larger bow. My studies, save for mathematics, do not prove too difficult. But First Communion calls for something quite different from these skills.

April 21, 1554

The new music teacher arrived. His name is Lorenzo Marcellini. He is most odd. He is afflicted with some nervous disorder and seems caught in a web of tics and twitches. He stutters and blinks rapidly. His face is a bit strange as well for he is slightly walleyed and his nose takes a sharp bend to the left. Oh well, he does play the cithara beautifully. And when he plays, all his tics and twitchings seem to dissolve. I am eager to resume my musical studies.

April 22, 1554

The weather, thankfully, has turned cool again. My portrait progresses. Between the posing for my portrait, the preparation for my First Communion, and my music lessons, in addition to my regular studies, I have hardly had any time for any of my favorite amusements, such as riding and hawking and practicing my archery on the larger bow. I shall not complain, though, for all these pursuits that I now do are most important for my moral development and my future duties as Queen. Clouet tells me that Queen Mary's father, Henry VIII, was a superb musician and a composer as well. He improved immensely the quality of court life through his devotion to the arts. The court life of Scotland and England has suffered from being regarded as coarse, uncivilized, and bordering on barbarism, at least in comparison with the French and Italian courts, which are considered the height of cultivation and devotion to the arts. So it is not idle for a Queen to spend her time in artistic pursuits. I have spoken to Signore Marcellini about my desire to learn musical composition. Perhaps I could set to music a poem that I write for Ronsard. I do want to write something of pure and lasting value. But right now I must actually turn my thoughts to my dear mother

and write her the news of my preparation for my First
Communion.

April 24, 1554

I think about the poison rumors that whirl about Queen
Catherine. I write this now and I pray no one ever discov-
ers this diary. But I must write in it. Perhaps if my mother
were here, I would not feel this way. I have my friends but
I have no mother to whom I can tell my most secret
thoughts and fears. A daughter and a mother have in a
sense a shared heart. There are still many things that I cannot disclose because of the distance from my mother, and
there are many things that a normal girl might disclose to
the hearts of her closest friends, but since I am a Queen I
cannot. Thus my diary has become my paper heart.

April 26, 1554

I am practicing having a good temper toward Signore
Marcellini. You see, Signore Marcellini, although not
nearly as vexing as Madame de Parois and Queen

Catherine, presents me with some problems. I do not particularly enjoy being in his presence. Not only does he twitch and his one eye seem to slide off the side of his face, but he also has a strong breath. Very cheesy breath. I cannot bear it when he leans over me and places his hands on top of mine to guide my fingers on the keyboard of the virginal. And yet he is a wonderful music teacher and he delights in my desire to learn composition. Not only that, he has invited the four Marys to join our lessons and promises to make us into a quintet with me on the virginal, Mary Beaton and Mary Livingston on the lute, and Mary Fleming and Mary Seton on the cithara.

April 29, 1554

I am getting much practice in developing good temper! First of all, Signore Marcellini seems to come often to work with me and the four Marys on our quintet. He is always suggesting practice times. And although I much prefer this to our ballet practices, he is here so much, and often lingers, until finally I feel it impolite if I do not invite him to stay for a cup of chocolate or cider. Janet Sinclair says I must always invite him, for he puts so much effort into our music lessons and he does not need to be teaching the four Marys as well, which he does only from the goodness of his own heart.

The second way in which I practice good temper is with my uncles. Since they have been here, my uncle the Cardinal and Uncle Francis have begun talking more and more about my marriage to Francis. In truth, I think — no, I know — they are fearful that because of his poor health he might die soon. I cannot bear the idea of losing him. I think of him not as an intended husband but as a dear friend. I can share the same sorts of thoughts and secrets with Francis as I do with the four Marys. How many boys can one do that with? He is like a brother to me but better. So although it disturbs me when my uncles speak of marriage, it disturbs me more that they do so because they fear for his life. I feel that across the bright light of our friendship slides the shadow of death. I shall be no more or less sad if I am, through Francis's death, left a widow or a maid without a friend. Death is death, and the loss will be incalculable whether I am married to him or not. So I do wish that my uncles would stop their talk. I know that all weddings amongst royal families have more to do with alliances and balances of power than love, but can they not let us have this friendship for now without casting these shadows upon it? It is true what Francis said that time when we were playing chess — that we are not so much children and sons and daughters of parents as we are pieces on a gigantic chessboard called Europe, that I am to be his in order to help checkmate England. I do wonder sometimes what it might be like to be ordinary — not a Princess or a Queen, but rather of simple birth, and to marry not to balance powers and check kingdoms but simply for matters of the heart. I think indeed I would still marry Francis, for he is so agreeable and of such a kind nature.

MAY 2, 1554

These are very secret thoughts that I now commit to these pages, but I must write them out, for indeed they have been haunting me since I last wrote in my diary. Until that moment when I wrote those words, wondering what it would be like to be of simple birth, I had never contemplated a notion of marriage for reasons other than those of state and politics and power and kingdoms. Now the thoughts sweep through my mind like the gusts of gale winds. My brain, nay, my heart as well, is in tumult. Francis is agreeable, and he is of kindest nature. Our minds are often as one when we study together or hunt or hawk or play, but I began to think, What if Francis were taller — as tall as, say, Robin MacClean, the head guardsman? I remember so well Robin carrying Mary Beaton ashore at Chenonceau. Water dripping from his huge shoulders. Icicles forming in his dark red beard. Will Francis ever grow a beard? His skin is as soft as mine. When I think these thoughts, I feel something stir deep inside of me. It is a feeling that is new to me. I know not what it is. But it is exciting and it makes my cheeks flush red. This much I know without looking in the mirror.

Two minutes later

Janet Sinclair just came in and blurted out, "Child, do you have a fever? You are bright red."

I nearly slammed shut my diary. This would be a giveaway and arouse curiosity. "Oh, no," I said. "I was just coughing." I then coughed. She seemed convinced. And then she said that Signore Marcellini was here for my music lesson. "Again!" I cried.

"Yes, he wants to prepare you for the Midsummer Night's feast." But I told her that this was the most ridiculous thing, for Midsummer Night is weeks off! And we shall not even be here but at Chenonceau or Amboise!

P.S. My portrait is nearly completed.

May 4, 1554

The weather has turned quite warm again, and now I am able to go to the great fountain for a picnic with the children, as Clouet no longer needs me that much for the portrait. Robin MacClean will accompany us and promises to bring a slingshot to teach us how to fling stones great distances.

Later

Horror! Signore Marcellini insisted on coming to our picnic. He arrived with his cithara and announced that music was the perfect accompaniment for a picnic. But, in fact, I do enjoy just the rustling of the leaves and the sound of the tumbling water of the fountain. He sat next to Mary Fleming, and I noticed that she was exceptionally quiet. I could not help but compare the men in our company. There was Lord Erskine and then Janet Sinclair's husband, John Kemp, both somewhat portly but men of fine posture and a hearty, easy manner. Then there was Francis. His skin perspired slightly and looked almost translucent. Color never seems to creep into his face on even the warmest days. His shoulders were hunched and his nose was running as usual. Then there was Signore Marcellini, all twitches and tics, stuttering and spilling his food on the cloth we had spread. It is evident he is not used to this French style of picnicking directly on the ground. And finally there was Robin MacClean leaning against the immense oak, his shoulders filling the breadth of the tree's trunk, a quiet grace to his posture. His face weathered with crinkly lines flaring out from his intense blue eyes that are always vigilant. My heart does race when I see him, and yet when I looked from him to Francis my heart nearly broke. I felt confusion.

So long I had looked forward to such a picnic and now I am filled with confusion.

MAY 6, 1554

Mary Fleming has been exceedingly quiet of late. It is unlike her character to be this quiet. I pray that everything is well with her.

My uncles returned to Meudon today. I sent with them a letter for Grandmama. I hope to visit there soon and see once more my little baby cousin and dear aunt. He has probably grown so much since his christening.

MAY 7, 1554

I have been working most diligently of late with Ronsard in writing couplets and then some quatrains. I think I am now ready to attempt a longer poem. Today I, by myself, went back to the grove where we had our picnic. Alone, I attempted to listen to the sound of the water as it tumbled and the whisper of the leaves. I wanted to still time and for one minute try to hear the strange music of eternity, for I do believe that this is from what poetry is created — lost moments recovered and made timeless.

MAY 8, 1554

We are required to attend the Queen tonight, as there is to be a musical concert given by Signore Marcellini and some other court musicians. Mary Fleming is not feeling well so she will not attend. She also missed our music class yesterday.

Something _is_ wrong with Mary but I am not sure if it

is simply a physical ailment. She is too quiet. The other Marys notice as well. I wish that King Henry would be here tonight for the musicale but he has followed Diane to Anet. There will be dancing after the concert, and the King is my favorite dance partner.

LATER

And you might imagine who is not my favorite dance partner — Signore Marcellini. He jerks about like a marionette with tangled strings. Oh, my goodness, I try so hard to be polite and kind but it is hard. I also danced with Monsieur d'un Humanieres. He is quite agile for a man of his age. Ronsard is a favorite partner. Francis told me he nearly collapsed laughing when he saw me with Signore Marcellini.

MAY 9, 1554

Days are full of lessons. Latin with George Buchanan, who is mightily irritated with Mary Beaton for her sloppy translations. Master Buchanan rarely becomes upset, so her work must have been exceedingly poor. He rolled his eyes toward the ceiling and muttered in Latin, which roughly translated meant, Cicero is turning in his grave. Signore Marcellini arrived for our music lessons with his hand bandaged. Mary Livingston asked him what had happened. He mumbled something about an unfortunate encounter with a book knife. But book knives are not that sharp. They are designed only to cut the paper of new books that come with their pages still fused. I detest being the first reader of a new book for just this reason. It takes so long to endlessly be cutting through the pages to read them.

May 12, 1554

Francis is ill again. I play endless games of chess with him. It rains. Mary Fleming grows more quiet each day. Mary Livingston cannot even come up with a funny ditty, and I struggle with my poem for Ronsard. We are all very tired of Fontainebleau. It is such a sad place in the rain. The blue slate from which it is built turns dark and forbidding. It is as if the entire château weeps in the rain. Our apartments have a stuffiness. Madame de Parois and the Italians chatter endlessly over their cups of hot chocolate. They do indeed gossip. I hear snatches of it all the time.

Oh, I hear a commotion and a bark from their game room. I must run.

Furious — absolutely furious. One of those friends of Madame de Parois kicked Thimble, who had trotted in and apparently began to nibble at one of the ladies' shoes. When I entered, little Thimble's mouth was bleeding! My demeanor must have been fearsome for a sudden silence fell on the room.

"Out! All of you out!" I wanted to call them names. But I would not indulge myself in such a display.

MAY 14, 1554

I am now sick in bed with a chest catarrh and feeling very feverish, my head throbbing, but I must write. After I had become so angry with Madame Parois' friends I had ordered Minette to fetch my Scots dress — my tunic of roughest linen, skins and breacans and *brats*, my high-lace boots. I tore off my hoop, dress, and kirtle. Minette helped me. "Where are you going, Your Majesty?"

"Out. Alone. Tell no one."

"Yes, Milady." Her eyes slid toward the window where rain was now beating down quite hard.

I picked up Thimble and tucked him under my *brat* where he would stay dry. I pulled my hair from its high, braided crown and let the single braid flow over my shoulder, slammed a tam on my head, and left.

High gusty winds made the driving rain slide across at a steep slant. I remember those many years ago when we sailed across the channel to France. The wind was against us one day so that the sailors were forced to take in sail and row across the channel. So, remembering those sailors, I furled my *brat* tight around me so it would not billow in the gusts and, tucking my head to my chest, I rammed diagonally across the wind.

My face was slick with rain by the time I reached the fountain, but I felt good. Then suddenly as I was sitting there in the rain cuddling Thimble beneath my *brat*, I heard a strange, unearthly sound with a beauty so intense I felt a bruise in my heart. It was the wild, lonely notes of a bagpipe! I had asked Lord Erskine to send pipers but they could not have yet arrived. The rain had almost ceased but vapor rose from the pool of the fountain and gathered in the old trees like moss turned to mist. For a moment I was completely confused. Had I suddenly become a spirit who could traverse two continents, hover within one moment in two different realms like some ghost queen? Then from the swirling mist a figure melted. My breath locked in my throat. Robin! Robin MacClean was piping those pipes, his *brat* thrown back over one shoulder. "Robin!" I cried out.

He ceased blowing on the pipes. "Your Majesty!" Indeed he was as surprised as I was. We knew not what to say to each other. I finally stammered an explanation of how I could not abide the courtiers chattering away. "Hence I seek peace and refuge here in this harsh weather." I gestured toward the sky.

"Not so foul, Your Majesty. In Scotland we would think nothing of this. Have you so forgotten Scotland?"

I felt the color rise in my cheeks, a sob swell in my throat. "Never!" My voice cracked. "What I would not give to be there now. I miss my mother most terribly and all about this court seems fusty and too ... too ..." But my voice dwindled.

"Aye, Milady, I understand." And his blue eyes shone

with feeling. Then he said something extraordinary to me, something I shall treasure forever. Something more precious than any gem in my jewel casket. "I look into Your Majesty's face and I believe that I am seeing Scotland. I believe the oceans evaporate and continents dissolve, and yes, I see my homeland."

He then began once more to play the pipes. He told me that he was practicing for when the Scots pipers arrive next month. He played for an hour, and I felt a peace steal over my soul, and yes, I felt the bruises in my heart. But to be bruised is to be human, to be coursing with blood. For bruises are caused by blood spilled under the skin. They are the tears that bleed inside. My eyes rested on Robin MacClean, and I have memorized every line of his face. I am shocked to have these feelings.

So now I am sick with the catarrh knocking in my chest. But I mind it not. I still hear the music Robin played. I can almost feel the mist on my cheek, and I remember the creases that fan out like rays of light from the edges of his bright blue eyes. It stirs my heart and my heart does pump blood and if I am to be bruised — well, so be it. I am human, a Queen now, and someday, a woman.

May 18, 1554

I am feeling better, but three of the four Marys are now sick. Not Mary Fleming. There is a part of me that wishes Mary Fleming were sick. It would perhaps explain some of her odd behavior. She was quite upset today when Madame de Parois insisted that even though the rest of us were sick that she continue with the music lessons with Signore Marcellini. I saw no need for it and thus have sent a note to Madame de Parois that there are to be no more music lessons until I can attend again.

June 1, 1554

Nearly two weeks since I have written. My illness took a turn for the worse. I was actually delirious at one point. They bled me. Doctor Bourgoing finally agreed. I was so delirious I did not realize they were slicing into my heel and cupping it. Now my heel is black and blue and hurts if I put weight on it. I had strange, turbulent dreams, for days on end it seemed. I often dreamed of Robin MacClean. In one dream we stood in a pool of the fountain and he piped to me. It was so real. I could almost feel the water lapping against my legs. In another we, Robin and I, were back in Scotland at

Lake Mentieth at the priory on the island of Inchmahome. We were the only people on the island, and Robin said we should swim around it. But I said, "I cannot swim."

"It is easy," he said. "I'll teach you how. Climb on my back." So I did. I held on to his broad shoulders, and the movement of his body through the water was soon inscribed on my mind, and I said, "I can swim by myself." And I slipped off his back and floated. We swam together around the island and on a rock near shore Francis waved to us. He had a sweet, sad look on his face.

"Oh, Mary! Mary! What a swimmer you are!" he called out.

"Come in, Francis. It's easy."

"No, I shall never be able to. Mary, you are strong and beautiful." I looked at Robin and I saw from the happy look on his face that he agreed. I hope that in my delirium I did not call out any names.

June 2, 1554

I prepare for a visit from the Bishop of Galloway along with a Scottish delegation. They bring letters, of course, from the rival factions and parties in Scotland. I fear that the Bishop will beg for mercy for the Duke of

Châtelherault, Lord Arran, who was found guilty of taking money from the treasury. It is, of course, unthinkable to restore his original powers, which he so abused. But I am not against mercy of some sort. I have discussed this in a letter to my mother and received from her yesterday a letter regarding this subject. It was one I had to hide most definitely from my uncle le Balafré. One might imagine what the old warrior thinks of any mercies being extended to anyone who has so abused his powers. Mother cautions me that I am of an impulsive nature and that I need only listen and give the appearance of an open mind. I need not come to a decision in the presence of these gentlemen. "Never," she wrote, "make a decision in public." I am to write her what indeed the proposals for mercy are, and then she shall deliberate and give me guidance on this matter. I have made a list of the important points of her letter concerning my demeanor during this audience right here in my diary. I destroyed the letter itself.

Things to remember when receiving the Bishop and the Scottish delegation:

Be attentive to each member of the delegation.

Look each gentleman directly in the eye as you speak to him.

Ask questions of as many gentlemen as possible, making sure to address each one by his full title (this I knew!).

At the end of the audience, I am to summarize briefly all that has been said — to prove that I listened — and then say the following words: "My Lords and Bishop, I have listened carefully to the subjects on which you have spoken. Be assured that I take these concerns most seriously and shall give them my considered thought. I thank you for your unflagging loyalty to the estates of Scotland."

And then I am to invite them to a special banquet at which my future husband, Francis, shall be in attendance. It is most important that Francis attend for this indeed will be a constant reminder of the vital connection between Scotland and France and the strong deterrent we shall present to the English.

June 5, 1554

Francis threw up at the banquet for the Scottish delegation! It splattered right onto the Bishop of Galloway's surplice! And then he — Francis, that is — fainted. This did not further the notion of the Scots-French alliance as a strong deterrent toward England. I was mortified. Of course, so was Francis. I tried my best to present an air of composure. But then I realized that perhaps this was wrong, as it might make them think that he does this all the time. And everything had gone so well until that point. I had done exactly as my mother counseled. When I write her a report of this meeting, I am not going to mention Francis's illness, although I probably should, for certainly the Scottish delegation will.

Concerning the mercies they requested on behalf of the Duke of Châtelherault, it was not as much as I had anticipated. They asked merely for a reduction of the interest on the money he is to pay back. I did as Mother said. I spoke neither yea or nay to such a proposal but gave them encouragement that I would consider it. Perhaps I did suggest that I felt this was not too much to ask.

I am completely exhausted, however, for I took much of the delegation hunting and hawking and horseback riding with me. I felt that I must make up for Francis in terms of my vigor. Poor Francis, he is in deepest despair. I keep telling him to pay no heed. It is done. It cannot be undone but people will forget it. But he sees through my words and says, "Mary, people do not forget when a Dauphin who is to be a King vomits at a state banquet." He is right but this I must not say.

I am absolutely furious. I thought the four Marys sympathetic to my embarrassment and predicament concerning Francis's illness at the banquet for the Scottish delegation. But then this morning I heard them all giggling madly as I entered Mary Fleming's chamber. I begged to be let in on the joke. They were suddenly quiet, and the more I insisted the more they hesitated. But I guessed immediately. "A new rhyme — tell me, Mary." So with eyes downcast she stepped forward and recited this loathsome ditty:

> *Francis sups with*
> *Kings and Lords*
> *Then brings it up in ways untoward.*
> *He burps*
> *He gags*
> *He turns bright red*
> *Then falls over*
> *As if he's dead.*

I absolutely boiled with anger. I fled the room and have not spoken to them all day.

June 8, 1554

We go to Anet in three days. The four Marys and I are so excited. Diane plans a masquerade ball for us. We are busy considering our costumes. Oh yes, I am finished being angry with the four Marys. It is hard to remain angry when there is so much good amusement to be had.

June 16, 1554
Anet

We are back at Anet and not a moment too soon. Queen Catherine, of course, is not with us, as she never comes here. I myself spent some days at Meudon visiting with Grandmama. The baby Charles has grown so. He now rolls over and smiles and reaches for objects you dangle in front of him. Aunt Anne and Grandmama both talk of how they hope that Queen Catherine will soon again be with child for it always improves her mood. She has lost more babies than I knew. This I never knew — that she was married nearly ten years before giving birth to Francis. I cannot imagine having babies. I mean, I know I want them, but somehow I picture them about four months old and very chubby and adorable like little Charles. Actually having them seems very mysterious to me, although I do know something about how that all comes about. The four Marys and I talk about it quite a bit.

Ronsard is also here with us at Anet. These are the days of Midsummer — the longest days of the year, the times of briefest darkness. It makes the nights slip by magically spun with starlight and moonlight between the dusk and the dawn. The dusk gathers from seven in the evening until nearly ten at night. It gives us a long twilight in which the world turns lavender, then a tender gray before the darkness thickens. That is why our masquerade ball shall not begin until an hour before midnight. We hope that the King will come. Oh, surely he will, for he loves dressing up with Diane and dancing under the stars.

With Ronsard we have studied much Greek and Latin literature in which the ancient pagan gods come out to frolic on this shortest night of the year. So we are all now deciding which deities and sprites and spirits we want to be. Janet Sinclair and her husband, John Kemp, and Lord Erskine plan to go as the three Fates who spin the thread of human destiny. Diane will undoubtedly go as her namesake, the goddess of the moon and the hunt, and if King Henry comes he will be Phoebus, the sun god. Francis is thinking of going as the Man in the Moon or Cupid with golden wings and a bow. Mary Seton wants to be Phillida, a shepherd girl. I want to go as Philomela, but everyone cries no, that her story is too sad. King Tereseus cut out her tongue for fear that she would tell his wife, her sister, that he loved Philomela more. He then abandoned her, telling everyone she was dead. But Philomela survived and was transformed into a nightingale who sang her story with a most beautiful voice. Master Cellini is here and shall help us with our costumes. He says he can design for me a most wonderful nightingale gown with jewel-studded wings and a feathered mask. Midsummer's Eve is only a few days away, so we must get to work.

JUNE 17, 1554

Everything here is almost perfect. Ronsard, Cellini, and all the wonderful artists of the court love Diane so. She holds poetry salons almost every evening. And if we are not in the music salon hearing Ronsard or some wonderful musician — not Signore Marcellini, whose talents show less brightly here — we are invited into her magnificent library, one of the finest collections in all of France, nay, all of Europe, some say. Many of the books are bound with golden arabesques and crimson velvet with enameled corners. She allows us all to take them down and read them.

In addition to these books, she has some very old, rare

manuscripts, one from the year 1358 — an unimaginable distance back in time. There is another written in the hand of an ancient Norman knight from the year 1422. She encourages all of us children to pore over these books and manuscripts. Diane is so different from Queen Catherine. The first phrase I learned in the court of France when I met Queen Catherine was, *Ne touche pas.* Don't touch. It is the first phrase I think all of the Queen's children learn. She is maniacally possessive of her things. She is consumed with fear that her precious books, or jewels, or whatever, shall be damaged. Diane is just the opposite. We are all so gay, except Mary Fleming, who grows more and more withdrawn every day. I think I must speak to her directly. The time has come.

June 18, 1554

Mary Fleming will say nothing. She asked me not to ask her anything and set her mouth firmly. It was as if her face had suddenly turned to stone. There was a steely look in her eye as if she might dare me as her Queen to command her to tell.

We have had our first fittings for our costumes. Mary Seton is a shepherdess. Mary Fleming is Titania, a nature sprite and Queen of the Fairies. Many thought I should be Titania, but you see, I am a real Queen and not a fairy one, so I do not think it proper to pretend to be a fantastical Queen. I am a nightingale, and if the story is too sad, well, people can make up another in their heads. Mary Beaton is Puck or sometimes he is called Robin Goodfellow, a mischievous sprite. Mary Livingston is a wood nymph. I love this holiday for it is twined with thoughts of magic and mischief and love — yes, it is a time for lovers and fire. Fire is believed to ensure a good harvest and fertility. In Scotland, farmers lead their sheep through villages and pastures with torches lighted from an immense Midsummer's bonfire. Some folk jump with their sweethearts over burning coals to prove their love because it is also a festival for lovers.

The four Marys and I plan to follow an ancient practice of which we have heard. We shall fast on the day of Midsummer Eve and lay a table in our apartments here at Anet with a clean cloth, bread, cheese, and wine and leave open our door. It is said that the spirit of the man one is to marry shall enter. Of course, it is not so exciting for me, as

I already know whom I am to marry. But I wonder if some magic might happen and suppose I were surprised and it was someone else's spirit and not Francis's. Oh dear, I should not write such things. I do love Francis so. But I think it is more exciting not knowing who you are to marry, as I have since I was four years old.

JUNE 21, 1554

Just a moment to write before I begin getting dressed for the masked ball. Oh, what a fine day we've had thus far on this Midsummer Eve. Diane herself came in and woke us up at dawn. She insisted that we all go riding to gather the flowers of Midsummer. We picked some mistletoe and bleeding heart, which grows in the thickest part of the forest that surrounds Anet, and then we went to the fields for lupine and cinquefoil and starflower. Diane tells us if we lay these flowers under our pillows on this eve we shall have dreams of love. So we rushed off and tore through the woods and meadows. Even Mary Fleming seemed a bit happier.

I can hardly write. Midsummer Night was not the eve of magic and love we so anticipated. If there was any magic, it was most dark indeed. We now know what has caused Mary Fleming's odd behavior. Signore Marcellini. For months now he has been trying to force his attentions on poor Mary, and last night as we played our Midsummer Eve games of chase and hide-and-seek through the garden mazes of Anet, he nearly succeeded. He jumped out of the hedge and nearly pounced on Mary Beaton, mistaking her in her costume for Mary Fleming. When he realized his mistake, he apologized lamely and scuttled off through the maze. Mary Beaton says it immediately came to her: There must have been something he said, a look in his eyes, she is not sure, but suddenly she realized that he thought she was Mary Fleming. She now understood Mary Fleming's anguish and sadness. Quickly she sought out Mary Fleming and took her to her apartment, where Mary said indeed she was right. Mary Beaton then went to fetch me and the other two Marys. We sat down at the very table we had set with the clean cloth, the bread, the cheese, and the wine, except we shut the door and did not leave it open for the spirit of our would-be sweethearts. Indeed as we sat down at the table to hear this horrid story, it struck me that this was a complete perversion of the magic and love that the eve was supposed to celebrate.

Here we sat, five terrified maidens, to hear a lurid tale of a sick old man and how he had made a living hell for our dear Mary Fleming. Luckily he never succeeded in kissing her. It must have been most revolting, but he did try to touch her where he should not. In fact that is how he came to "cut" his hand with a "book knife." It was not a cut but a bite from Mary's teeth! I said I would immediately see to having him dismissed. But Mary Fleming protested that he is a favorite of Queen Catherine's, and that in any case, he would deny everything and then make her look bad and Queen Catherine is already so set against Mary Fleming because of her mother. "Signore Marcellini," she spoke in a quavering voice, "has told me that this is to be our little secret, and that if I dare say anything, he shall tell everyone that I am just like my mother in my wanton behavior. And you know how much the Queen hated my mother. Oh, I am finished, Mary," she cried. "You must send me back to Scotland. It is the only way."

"Never!" I replied. "Why should you have to pay for his foul behavior?"

Then Mary Beaton spoke up. Her eyes narrowed in thought as she spoke. "We must catch him. If we witness it, we shall have undeniable evidence."

We all fell silent, and as I looked around the table at the four Marys, I realized that this was perhaps not simply five young maids all named Mary, but in a sense this was my first council of war. I listened carefully. I was now weighing in my mind what Mary Beaton had said. I could not be impulsive.

I realized that the best sovereigns, whether on the battlefield or in the council of the privy chambers of the estates, make decisions with both their heads and their hearts. Wisdom and justice must always be tempered by the most human of instincts. So I turned to Mary Fleming. "If we proceed in this way, Mary, it will mean more discomfort and anguish for you, at least temporarily. What think you of this?"

"Your Majesty." The four Marys rarely address me in such a formal way so I knew that indeed I was becoming a sovereign before their eyes. "I have been wrong."

I cut her off. "You have not been wrong, Mary. You are the victim, not the culprit. It is his shame, not yours."

"Yes, Your Majesty, I understand, but what I was going to say is that I was wrong in not telling you all, my dearest friends, sooner. My anguish is already relieved for the telling, and now with you beside me I think that I can tolerate this temporary discomfort."

We all agreed that we would then proceed as Mary

Beaton had recommended. We shall try to trap Signore Marcellini.

July 12, 1554
Chambord

We are back at Chambord. So far we have not had an opportunity to lay our trap. The next day after the Midsummer Eve, Signore Marcellini was summoned to Blois by Queen Catherine. Since we have once more settled in here at Chambord he has been seen little. We have had precious few music lessons. Of course, it is the height of summer and our activities are mainly out of doors.

My old hawk Ruffles is ailing. It seems that after his last molt of feathers he contracted some illness. He has unsightly bare spots that we must dab with olive oil to soothe the irritation. Monsieur Gilbert, the hawk master in the mews, is hopeful that old Ruffles shall fly again. Francis is quite dear with Ruffles, bringing him tasty morsels from the kills of his own hawks. And not only that, but he also lets me fly his newest falcon, Sebastian. I think hawking is one of the things that Francis and I do well together. Our instincts combined with those of the birds seem to fit perfectly when we are in the field. We speak very little to each other but silently give the calls to the birds and perform our hand signals. This afternoon the two of us went out with only Robin MacClean as our guard. And I thought as I took a rest on the ridge of a hill that there was something of perfect harmony amongst the three of us and the birds we had brought to fly. If only all of life could be kept in the company of such good souls. But I am blessed with an abundance of good company, for do I not also have the four Marys?

I considered telling Francis about the problem of Signore Marcellini. He would love to be in on the plot to entrap the foul creature, and I daresay he would put a good twist on it — come up with something quite imaginative. But I cannot tell Francis, for it could put him at risk. His mother is always snooping into his business, and he might be forced to say something to her, and then our plans would surely be dashed. The Queen is exceedingly fond of Signore Marcellini. Oh yes, the Queen is most definitely with child. It has been confirmed. The baby will come sometime in early spring. Little Princess Marguerite, who just turned one last May, is becoming the most engaging infant. She is full of charm and smiles and is always of a good nature, unlike little Henry. I cannot understand how the Queen can dote on that boy the way she does. Although he is only three, there is something devious about him.

June 15, 1554

René the Florentine has arrived and brought my perfume! It is perfect. And unlike the Queen I plan to share mine with the four Marys and not simply covet it. I dabbed some on a handkerchief and passed it amongst them, and they all grew misty eyed. These four girls have come so far from their homeland for so long simply to be with me in my little court, how can I deprive them of this bit of Scotland?

Michel Nostradamus has also arrived to do the astrological charts and predictions for Queen Catherine's new babe.

July 16, 1554

It seems that all of Scotland is coming to me now. My bagpipers have at last arrived. I plan to give a *petit bal* to celebrate, and the four Marys and I shall wear our new perfume and new gowns. We are devising our trap for

Signore Marcellini at the *petit bal*. We have a plan in which Mary Fleming will feign lightheadedness and seek some fresh air on a private balcony. We shall already be outside, the four of us hidden behind the huge pots in which the lime trees grow. She plans to do this after the second gavotte — the Burgundian version of the dance requires much jumping about, so one might actually become faint.

JULY 19, 1554

The *petit bal* was a delight. But our trap did not work. I am wondering if Signore is suspicious. Maybe his encounter with Mary Beaton stopped him. I am not sure. We shall continue to watch for more opportunities.

The bagpipers were excellent and Robin MacClean played with them. Signore Marcellini, of course, hated the music. Queen Catherine came for a brief time and arranged her face into a tense smile as they played. I could see that she did not like the music either. But King Henry loved it. He asked me if he might "borrow the pipers" to entertain the Spanish delegation that is expected shortly. There are more rumors that a match is to be arranged between Princess Elizabeth, or perhaps even Princess Claude, and a member of the Spanish royal family. I worry for them both, as we understand that the Spanish court is quite backward. They lack any refinements of the arts or culture that we enjoy here. Their courts are full of intrigue, and their bishops enjoy excessive amounts of power and are known to be cruel and harsh. It seems that the main business of Spain is the Inquisition and the rooting out of Jews. They devote themselves to this task almost exclusively. I do wonder what these envoys from the Spanish court will think of our court's Jew, the astrologer Michel Nostradamus. Actually there are many Jews here in the court who fled Spain and now serve the King and Queen.

JULY 24, 1554

There is a flurry in the court. Rumors of a prophesy by Nostradamus have leaked out and it does not bode well. The expected baby is fine and a brilliant life is predicted. Nostradamus says it a boy. This, of course, makes the Queen very happy. But then people who are privy to the Queen's innermost circle have reported that the Queen began to press Nostradamus further concerning other predictions, and now it is said that he has prophesied the early death of dear King Henry. It is an obscure quatrain, and I am not sure why it is necessarily interpreted as the death of Henry, but the verse has made its rounds through the court. It goes as follows:

The young lion shall overcome the old one
In martial field by a single duel
In a cage of gold he shall put out his eye
Two wounds from one, then he shall die a cruel death.

The King is said to be mightily upset but not because of his death being predicted. He believes astrologers provide nothing but nonsense. I have heard him say so on many occasions, but he is most worried that it will disturb Queen Catherine and her pregnancy, which has been going so well. He has been most solicitous of the Queen. He did not even come to Anet for the Midsummer Eve ball of Diane de Poitiers, for he knew it would upset the Queen. I hope he doesn't send Nostradamus away. We quite enjoy him. Mary Beaton and René the Florentine, Nostradamus, and myself have enjoyed several games of tennis in this fine weather.

JULY 26, 1554

I had the strangest sensation today when I returned to my apartments from riding. I had the feeling that someone had rearranged the things on my writing desk. Of course, I never leave my diary out. Indeed I hide it away in a locked box for which only I have the key. There are certain letters and papers from my mother also in this box.

JULY 29, 1554

I had the same feeling once more today. I have been thinking hard. Is it my imagination? Feelings, sensations like this are so slippery and yet they can drive you mad. I do not know how anyone could gain access to my apartments. Janet Sinclair has a receiving chamber just outside the apartments. She can see everyone who goes by. Minette, my chambermaid, is the only one with free entry, and she is about most of the time. When she is not tending to me directly, she is tending to my wardrobe, either sewing on buttons or making alterations. The dogs yap at the slightest intrusion, especially Thimble, who has somewhat of a nervous temperament.

I disclosed to Mary Beaton my thoughts that my personal things, particularly on my writing desk, have been disturbed. This writing desk goes with me to each château. I am particularly fond of it, and although I keep my most personal correspondence in my locked box, I do have some papers in the drawers here. I explained all this to Mary. She thought for a moment, then suddenly plucked a hair from her head. "What in the name . . ." I caught myself, for I must not use the Lord's name in vain. "What are you doing?" I asked as she began to thread the hair through the latch of one of the desk's small compartments.

"If the hair is broken," she replied, "you will definitely know someone has been looking in these small drawers and cubbies." What a wonderful idea! Mary Beaton is so smart. It is truly regrettable that a female can never serve in the Privy Council of a Queen. Mary Beaton would have so much to offer.

AUGUST 1, 1554

Ha! The hair has been broken. Someone does tamper with my things. Now to catch the wrongdoer. Mary Beaton suggested that we leave something tantalizing that the person will want to have, some piece of information. Something that we could catch him or her with. I would not put it beyond Madame de Parois to tamper here. She is always so interested in how much the yardage and the embroideries for my gowns cost, and I am given copies of all such bills. But Mary Beaton says no, that the person would not risk the danger of being discovered for the sake of a few bills. There are easier ways to find out such things. I suppose she is right. I hope we are more successful in laying this trap than we were with the one for Signore Marcellini. He has made himself quite scarce of late, and Mary Fleming seems much happier. We go to Blois in a few days. The river is down, so it is not certain that we will be able to go by barge. If indeed we must move by carriages it will be very hot and dusty.

AUGUST 7, 1554
BLOIS

That little brat Henry! He is growing more impossible every day. He pushed the darling Marguerite down a flight of steps and she cut her lip. Luckily Robin MacClean was right by and scooped up Marguerite and took her directly to the nursery. The doctor was called. But when Robin returned, he gave little Henry a good talking to. His Scottish burr crept into his French and thickened it. Little Henry, who is nearly four, screamed and called for his mama. "I am going to tell my mama on you. I shall be King someday and I shall put you in prison." I stepped forward at that moment and said, "Henry, Francis shall be King and I shall be his Queen and I already am Queen of the Scots, and you must stop this blathering right now and apologize to Robin MacClean." He ran off wailing.

Robin MacClean winked at me and said, "Thank you, Milady. I fear it's hopeless with that one." I fear he is right, but it was almost worth it just for the wink. How my heart did melt. Of course, it was not worth it to have dear little Marguerite's lip cut. But Marguerite is a plucky child. I really have no fears for her.

AUGUST 9, 1554

Mary Beaton and I were discussing how to catch the desk rifler. I told Mary how my mother sometimes sends me false letters to give to my uncle Francis de Guise, because he is so nosy about our business. I swore her to absolute secrecy. Mary suggested that I take one of the recent false letters and place it in one of the drawers of the writing desk and see if the person takes it. I protested that surely the person would not take it for it would be noticed immediately. Mary said that of course I was right but that there still must be a way. We thought hard but could not come up with anything. If we could just catch the person doing it. "Perhaps," I said, "we could put something on the paper that would . . ." I did not complete my thoughts.

"That's it," Mary said. "Remember when we were playing tennis with Doctor Nostradamus and he was telling of the invisible powders?"

"But, Mary," I protested, "we need something visible. Some unmistakable sign that will leave traces and lead us to the culprit."

Mary jumped up from the plump cushions she sat on. "We don't know what this might be, but surely Doctor Nostradamus might. We must consult with him immediately."

I think she is right about this, although I am not sure if Nostradamus will want to become involved. He serves at the favor of the Queen, not me. But I suppose there is no harm in asking.

August 13, 1554

We have sought out Nostradamus, and there is indeed a powder that he can make us. One dampens the paper just slightly with a sponge, not enough to make the ink run. Then the powder is sprinkled on. It immediately dissolves into the paper, and any hands that touch the paper will be streaked with purple in twenty-four to forty-eight hours. We must be careful to douse our own hands in a resinous juice he will give us that comes from Palestine and is called myrrh. This will protect our hands from the powder so they will not turn purple. So we are set to catch a snoop. Such people in my mind are of the same evil rank as hypocrites.

August 15, 1554

Mary Beaton and I have decided on the "bait," which letters to put into the writing compartment. There is one from my mother that advises me on Lord Arran concerning his fines and punishments. It is precisely the sort of letter a spy might want to lay his hands on. It contains no significant information, which is why she wrote it as a cover for me to show Uncle Francis. The real letter was much more specific and told me whom to beware of in the court and who might be plotting for the benefit of Lord Arran. The second letter I shall use is from me to mother concerning Mary Fleming, in which I write that Mary seems less sad and withdrawn but that I do wish her mother could return to France.

AUGUST 16, 1554

The bait has been placed. We have threaded the hair through the latch. We wait.

AUGUST 17, 1554

The hair is still unbroken.

AUGUST 18, 1554

Still unbroken.

Broken! The two letters were replaced exactly as we had left them. Now we wait.

I go for my final fitting for the gown I am to wear to the Pleiades ball. This is the liveliest ball of the season. It celebrates the seven greatest poets of France, known as *la Pléiade*. The ball is always held in late August for this is the time of the shooting stars, and it seems most fitting to have a grand celebration of these poets. They shall all be here, I think, except for perhaps Jean Antoine de Baif, who suffers from gout. It is an evening that shimmers with starlight and poetry. I plan to wear a white damask gown that is appliqued with small seed pearls in the form of the constellation of the Pleiades. This was my own idea. At my throat I shall wear the star sapphire brooch given to me by my grandmama. On my head I plan to wear what we call a Scottish cap. It is made of white satin and worn at a tilt so it swoops low on one side. There is a rosette of ostrich feathers sewn on and around the edges are gold letters with my title in Latin, *Mariae, Reginae, Scotorum*. It is my most dazzling costume ever, my homage to the greatest poets in France and, most likely, Europe. I cannot wait for the ball. I have requested that the other four Marys not wear white, but, of course, we shall all wear the wonderful perfume that René devised for us.

The ball is just two days away. I can hardly wait.

AUGUST 20, 1554

Twenty-four hours have passed but no one shows purple hands.

AUGUST 21, 1554

Forty-eight hours have passed. No, forty-nine, but no traces of purple. I begin to get ready for the ball. It is a lovely evening, but Mary Beaton and I wonder why the powders have not worked.

AUGUST 23, 1554

The powders worked! I take not the name of the Lord in vain when I say, My God, how shocked and frightened I was. I must now ask if it was worth it. Never would I have expected the events to unfold as they did and right at the ball at that. My exquisite dress ruined — stained with purple! My dear Mary Fleming's face bruised with the same purple, the bodice of her dress and the top of her breasts hideously splotched purple, and that is not all! Let me directly as possible relay the events and then reveal the culprit.

All four Marys and I had been at the ball for at least an hour or more. We had dined on fruit ices and sweet pastries that were cut into the shapes of stars. The poets delighted us with recitations. A quadrille had been called and then a gavotte, a Burgundian one. I did not notice, nor did any of us, really, although apparently Mary Fleming thought she had caught Mary Seton's and Mary Livingston's eye when she left the ballroom. There was another dance or two and then the Paduan pavane, a favorite of the Italians, as it comes from the city of Padua. Signore Marcellini had taught it to me and I thought nothing of his asking to be my partner. In the Paduan version of the pavane, the gentleman places his right hand on the lady's waist and spins her slowly clockwise and then counterclockwise before they proceed for sixteen counts side by side, with his hand still on her waist. We did this, and then when the dance was completed I curtsied to Signore Marcellini, as is the custom. He left.

The next dance I was partnered with the poet Joachim Du Bellay. First of all, it must be understood that Du Bellay had arrived only that afternoon and secondly that the dance we did had no touching. We merely faced each other. At the finish as I dipped down in my curtsy I saw these odd streaks across the bodice of my dress. They were purple streaks! The hands that touched my waist had touched the letters! My partner in the last dance, the Paduan pavane, was the snoop, none other than Signore Marcellini!

Just as these separate thoughts began to weave themselves into a web of horror, there was a tiny yelp, almost as if a dog had been stepped on. It was a cry from the balcony off the ballroom. I don't think many others heard it, but I saw Mary Beaton's face white with fury. I rushed to the balcony. Mary Beaton dragged me to the shadows where Mary Livingston and Mary Seton stood with their arms around Mary Fleming. Her face was bloodless except for the streaks of purple that slashed like saber marks across one cheek and down her neck to where her bodice had been torn and hung stained with purple. Her lips, too, were purple, making her mouth appear like a squashed blossom.

We all stared at one another and then the girls looked at me. "Your dress, Mary!" Of course, only Mary Beaton knew about the purple powder and the trap we had set to catch the snoop, but we had no idea that the snoop would be the loathsome creature Signore Marcellini! At that moment we saw Signore Marcellini threading his way through the back of the ballroom and furiously peeling off his gloves. But his hands were bright purple, as well! I raced to pick up a glove as it fell. "Mary Beaton," I said sharply, "explain to the other Marys what is happening. I am off to see Queen Catherine directly." The Queen had retired earlier.

"Is that wise, Your Majesty?" Mary Beaton bobbed a half curtsy. Did she perhaps mean it was impulsive? Would my mother have counseled me to wait, to reflect before acting? But I could not. I was outraged and the evidence was here. I was told by the Queen's steward that she was in her paneled cabinet room — the room where behind the 237 carved panels Queen Catherine keeps her jewels, her state papers, and some say her poisons.

Two guards stood outside. "I am here to see the Queen on business of utmost urgency," I announced.

"She is resting."

"She must see me." There was silence. Then from behind me another voice said, "Did you not hear the Queen of Scots?" I wheeled around. It was Robin MacClean. He had followed me. He looked most savage next to these guards in their silken hose and gold-embroidered waist-coats and doublets. Their chapeaus were festooned with feathers, like mine. I despise men in feathers.

They immediately announced me, and I walked through the immense doors. Queen Catherine stood with her back to me. She appeared small and erect. Her head was bowed down as she spoke still with her back to me. "So what do you seek, Little Queen?" She turned slowly around to me. My fist tightened on the glove I held as I saw what the Queen had been looking at with her bowed head. Her own plump fingers were bright purple.

There were really no words exchanged. I merely held up the glove and said, "I believe that this belongs to your spy, Signore Marcellini. He has also left the mark of his lust on the breast and face of Mary Fleming." The Queen blanched and then sank to the floor.

That is all that I write now. It is an eerie time here in the court.

August 24, 1554

Signore Marcellini has been summarily dismissed. The Queen is believed to be suffering another miscarriage. I now must hope that I am not in some way blamed. Lord

Erskine stays by my side ready to advise me in all matters. At this time a letter has also been written to my mother to advise her to release Madame de Parois of her service in my household. She is a troublemaker. Lord Erskine, my dear guardian, tells me that I should have told him immediately of the problem of Signore Marcellini and his harassment of Mary Fleming. It is difficult for me to explain to him why I did not, but there is something so embarrassing about it. I remember when a servant girl, the chambermaid before Minette, had some trouble with a groomsman. It was difficult for me to believe because she was like a mouse and almost frightened of her own shadow. I could never believe that she would have invited someone's attentions, as people said she had. I didn't want Mary Fleming to be subjected to this kind of gossip and blame. It seems so unfair. I don't think she will be, now that everyone knows the truth about Signore Marcellini. Indeed the only person who might inspire blame is myself for agitating Queen Catherine to the point of miscarrying yet again. I pray that I do not invite the wrath of the King. He was at Anet with Diane and is now coming here. I must bide my time until he gets here and pray for his understanding. In the meantime I seek counsel with my Father Confessor. I am surrounded by good people. They love me and they know that I have tried to act with a sense of compassion and integrity in the best interests of innocent people. That is all I can do, God willing.

August 26, 1554

The King arrives tomorrow. I am so nervous I pray a great deal. I work on my Latin translations. I study my catechism. I cannot go near my lute for the foul memories it recalls of my music lessons. I must get over this. I must not let that vile man ruin music for me. Indeed that would be his final triumph.

September 1, 1554

Diane first came to see me, before the King. She told me he is not angry with me at all but indeed is perturbed with the Queen. He apparently roared at the Queen and asked why she would spy on our dear little Scottish queen. Well, I am relieved.

September 2, 1554

I have met with the King. He has extended his deepest sympathies for the terrible anguish I have suffered and *la petite* Mary Fleming. He asked me repeatedly if she is in good health but turned red whenever he tried to get out the next words. Diane spoke for him. She began delicately. "The King wishes to know if little Mary Fleming's honor has been damaged in any way."

"Oh, no, Madame."

The King then sank with relief into a chair.

I am pleased that it has gone this way with the King, and very pleased that Diane de Poitiers came with him. I plan to leave this court for a while. I do not want to leave the Marys behind, so I sent a letter to my uncles saying that we would all like to come and visit them and Grandmama at Meudon for a spell.

September 10, 1554

Word arrived today that we are all to go to Meudon. I am so excited. We shall spend a fortnight there. It is a lovely time of year. We plan just to play. No lessons. There is not room to bring all the tutors along, so only Janet Sinclair and Lord Erskine will accompany us.

September 16, 1554
Meudon

We have been at Meudon these past three days, and it has been heaven without the horrible Signor Marcellini. The four Marys and I have rediscovered our love of music here. I have taken up the lute again and Mary Beaton and Mary Seton the lyre, and a servant has brought in the virginal that Mary Fleming and Mary Livingston both play. We spend hour upon hour playing airs much to Grandmama's and my uncle's and aunt's delight.

September 17, 1554

I continue to prepare for my First Communion, which is less than a month away. Grandmama presented me with her rosary. This is such a big step. I hope I am fully prepared.

September 18, 1554

We received word that the King and Queen have been making a grand royal progress through France. This is the first time in some years to visit his kingdom from village to village and province to province. He would like me and the four Marys to join the progress at Lyon. How exciting. None of us has ever been to Lyon, which is a center of silk factories and printing presses. We are to join the King on the royal barge, but not Queen Catherine. She travels on a separate barge in a few days.

September 21, 1554
Aboard the King's royal barge one mile from Lyon

The current is swift so we shall very shortly be there and we see throngs of people lining the banks. The vineyards are russet colored this time of year, as the harvest nears. The barge will pull to the riverside, and the King shall mount his charger to make his way along the road into the center of the city of Lyon.

LATER

The four Marys and I followed King Henry on our little Scotch ponies. The townspeople were delighted when they saw us. They have never seen horses like these, so small but pretty and strong. The Grand Seneschal, the highest court judge of France, and various dignitaries of the city along with the members of guilds representing the silk merchants and printers were marching with their banners to greet the King. There were trumpets blasting and pennants snapping in the breeze. The crowds that lined the way roared and cheered as we passed. But the best was yet to come. As we came to the city, amidst the rooftops and the chimneys, right in the town square, a forest seemed to grow. It was an artificial one that had been planted, and standing in the groves of trees were lovely girls all dressed as Greek goddesses and in hunting costumes of black and white with crescent moons in their hair. It was, of course, a tribute to Diane de Poitiers. The city of Lyon is very near to her duchy and childhood home.

The crowd went wild when the King leaned over and took Diane's hand and raised it on high. The people of Lyon adore Diane, and one could see that the King reveled in their adoration. Mary Seton leaned over from her pony and whispered, " 'Tis lucky Queen Catherine is not seeing this."

"But she will soon enough," I replied, for indeed custom dictates that on these royal progresses the Queen enter a town separately after the King with her own ranks of soldiers. Finally it was time for Queen Catherine's litter to enter. It was covered in gold brocade. I had not seen the Queen since that fateful night when she stood in her cabinet room, her hands stained purple. She sat atop the litter now, gleaming in the finest Lyonnaise silk and jewels. She smiled brightly even as she went beneath the arches topped with the symbols and emblems of Diane, the crescent moon and the bow of the hunting goddess. How could she maintain that brittle smile when it was so obvious that the one celebrated here was not the Queen of France but Diane the Huntress? For a moment, despite all, I felt a twinge in my heart. To be so ugly and unloved. No wonder she resorts to scheming and bitter intrigues. And look at Diane. Tall, slender, forever beautiful and regal. There was a part of me that I think wanted to feel sorry for Catherine, wanted to forgive her, but then something locked in my heart.

October 5, 1554
Meudon

I have been called back to Meudon. Grandmama is desperately ill. She has received the Last Rites, and I now sit by her bed. I hold her hand, and the rosary she gave me is entwined between both our fingers. Some terrible paroxysm felled her. Her face is skewed sideways into a strange grimace. The left side of her body does not move. One eye is shut and the other open in an icy stare. We know not if she hears us or even recognizes us.

October 10, 1554

One endless day follows another. Grandmama does not improve, nor does she grow worse. For that we are thankful. It is hard to write. I do nothing except sit by her bed. My First Communion has been delayed. I had always imagined Grandmama present for it. Now I can hardly think about it.

October 15, 1554

No change.

October 21, 1554

Still the same. I miss the Marys and Francis.

November 15, 1554

Grandmama moved today! She moved and muttered something! We are wild with excitement. The doctor says that this has been known to happen with victims of a stroke. All of us keep a constant vigil now by her bed.

November 17, 1554

Grandmama spoke. She spoke my name this morning at 11:00. It sounded strange, as if she had a thick paddle in her mouth instead of a tongue, but everyone recognized that she called my name. Then her eyes opened. The one that had been clenched so tight and that side of her face began to relax. We are having a Mass of thanksgiving this morning. My uncle the Cardinal and Father Mamerot shall lead us.

NOVEMBER 20, 1554

Grandmama's recovery is miraculous. Today she sat up in bed for the first time. She can speak but sometimes her words are mixed together wrongly and her tongue is still thick in her mouth.

NOVEMBER 21, 1554

Guess what Grandmama asked today? When my Communion is. We are now thinking of having it on my birthday at Saint-Germain-en-Laye, if Grandmama is well enough to travel.

NOVEMBER 29, 1554

Grandmama walks and talks. Her left side still is very weak. I am excited to see my dear Marys and Francis again soon.

December 7, 1554
Saint-Germain-en-Laye

It is one day before my birthday and almost a year ago that I began this diary that my dear mother sent to me all the way from Scotland. I once again stand on the roof garden of the château and watch the river flow below me. I began my fast a few hours ago. It is an ancient practice. Many do not do it before their First Communion, but I decided to, for it is said that through fasting one can seek a purity of heart. This I need in order to be a true communicant. I want to remember the hunger in my stomach each time I take the sacraments, for with this in mind, with a purity of heart I shall, I think, be a better Christian as well as a good Queen. I need to do this for I know that there is within my heart a dark part. I am not sure precisely what the cause is, but there is a shadow that lurks there. I want this shadow to dissolve before I kneel before the altar and recite the catechism to my confessor. What is it that lurks in my heart? What could it be? I search and search for it. Perhaps the hunger will drive it out.

I think indeed I drifted to sleep up here on the roof garden. The wind whips around the chimneys. There is a pit in my stomach so hollow it makes a rumbling noise. Tomorrow there will be a feast following my Communion to be attended by Grandmama and my uncles and the four Marys, Ronsard, my tutors, Francis, Princesses Elizabeth and Claude and of course King Henry and the Queen.

NEAR MIDNIGHT, DECEMBER 7, 1554

I have just come back from retrieving my diary from the roof garden. I threw it down when it suddenly came to me the source of the inscrutable shadow that darkened the edges of my heart. It was the Queen in a sense. She did not cause the shadow, but it was my own selfishness and pinched spirit toward her that made the shadow hover in my heart. When I realized this, I threw down my diary and raced down flights of stairs searching out Queen Catherine. I had not seen her since my return from Meudon. She was in her Salon of Reception. Once more I demanded of the guards that I be allowed to see the

Queen. And when they hesitated, I was surprised once more by that voice, the Scots burr creeping through to roughen the French. "Did you not hear the Queen of Scots?" It was Robin MacClean. He had followed me. Indeed he had probably guarded me the entire time I was on the roof.

In a softer voice I said to the guard, "Tell Her Majesty that I beg to see her."

And so I was admitted. The Queen seemed surprised. I curtsied deeply.

The words at first were hard. I thought of my grand-mama and that heavy paddle of a tongue that stirred the words like thickest batter, but I spoke them. "I humbly beseech Your Majesty and my future mother-in-law." I heard the Queen gasp. The word "mother" must have sounded strange coming from my lips but I continued. "That tomorrow at my ceremony of Communion you stand in the chapel beside me and on the other side my grandmama."

An absolute hush fell over the chamber. I could hear the breathing of her ladies-in-waiting. I heard the rustle of one searching for her smelling salts. "You would do me such an honor," I said in a strong voice. I felt the shadow dissolve. I knew now that I was truly prepared to receive the sacraments. For to submit to a greater power, the power of God, one must banish the smallness in one's soul. I was at last ready for Communion and ready to rule, for in this end of selfishness was my true beginning as a sovereign. I was truly Mary, Queen of Scots.

EPILOGUE

On Sunday, April 24, in the year 1558, just a few months short of her sixteenth birthday, Mary Stuart married Francis, the Dauphin of France. The ceremony, which took place in the cathedral of Notre Dame in Paris, was one of unequaled splendor and Renaissance pageantry. To signify her new position as wife of the future King of France, a new crown embedded with rubies, pearls, and sapphires was placed on Mary's head. At one point during the banquet that followed, her head and slender neck began to ache under the weight of the crown, and King Henry directed his own Lord-in-waiting to remove it. Some people took it as an omen of the future of the vulnerable and soon-to-be-embattled young Queen of the Scots.

In November 1558, scarcely seven months after Mary's marriage to Francis, Mary Tudor, Queen of England, died, leaving no heirs. Her half-sister, Elizabeth, became

Queen. Elizabeth was unmarried. Some thought that Elizabeth was not a legitimate heir to the throne of England since her father's divorce from his previous wife was never recognized by the Catholic Church. Thus his marriage to Elizabeth's mother was considered invalid. So, immediately upon the death of Mary Tudor, Mary Stuart's father-in-law, Henry II of France, proclaimed that his daughter-in-law, Mary, was the Queen of not only Scotland but also of England. Such a move hardly endeared Mary to Elizabeth or the people of England. She could be viewed only as a usurper. This declaration became the first stroke in what would ultimately become a deadly design.

LIFE IN FRANCE
1553

HISTORICAL NOTE

The sixteenth-century world of Mary, Queen of Scots was dominated by two extraordinarily powerful influences — the Renaissance and the Reformation. Both were movements that inexorably changed how humans viewed themselves in relation to the world and the societies in which they lived. The Renaissance, which literally means "rebirth" or "renewal of life and vigor," was a renewal of learning and *really* reached its zenith during that century. It is considered to be a time of the greatest artistic achievement in Western Europe. Artists such as Leonardo da Vinci and Michelangelo, and poets such as Dante and Ronsard, flourished. New ways of thinking and new standards of thought, of beauty, and of artistic creation were introduced. Humans became central to many of these new values. Humanity was to be celebrated through art and architecture. Florence, Italy, home of Catherine de Medici, was considered one of the foremost centers of creativity during the Renaissance, and Catherine de Medici was indeed responsible for introducing into the French court arts, such as ballet, and fashion trends, such as high heels and perfume.

It was during the sixteenth century that the Catholic Church and the Pope had weakened as symbols of spiritual unity in Europe. Plagued by corruption and greed, the Church had lost much of its prestige. Because of this loss of influence, it became easier for new ideas to be introduced, ideas that emphasized the central value of humans and their potential to create lasting things on earth. At the same time Protestant reformers who had objected to the worldliness and corruption of the Church gained strength. It was during this century that Martin Luther and John Calvin began a religious revolution that became known as the Reformation. On October 31, 1517, Luther posted his ninety-five theses on the door of a church in Wittenberg, Germany. The theses criticized the Catholic Church's practice of selling indulgences and stressed the spiritual inward character of the Christian faith. The posting of the theses to the church door is thought of as the beginning of the religious Reformation. Martin Luther's reform ideas began to spread throughout Europe. By 1550, Lutheranism was a major force in northern Europe. In Scotland, men such as John Knox were rejecting the Catholic Church and Catholic monarchs, in attempts to make the country a Protestant one. The Protestantism that Knox established in Scotland — the Presbyterian faith — made possible the eventual union of Scotland with England. In England, Queen Elizabeth practiced a religious tolerance that found favor with the reformers.

So the world into which Mary Stuart was born was one in which old orders were giving way to new ones. Art and humanism were becoming important. Religion and its connections with politics was being questioned. Monarchies were still strong, but the first hints that a separation of church and state might be advisable, that religious tolerance might be a good policy, were emerging. The culture was becoming more secular, and the people did not trust the old religion of the medieval era. Still, not all were ready for the Protestantism of the reform.

Henry VIII, angry with the Pope who would not give him a divorce from his wife, Catherine of Aragon, did not embrace Luther or the reform movement but began his own church, the Church of England. His daughter, Mary Tudor, a devout Catholic, incensed by her father's abandonment of the Church and her mother, during her reign became militant in her attempts to follow her faith. She ordered thousands of heretics (her word for anyone who was not a practicing Catholic) burned. Her sister, Elizabeth, however, when she became queen declared that she did not want to "open windows in men's souls," meaning that she did not care to peer into people's private religious beliefs.

When Luther's works first appeared in Paris, King Francis I, father of Henry II, banned them. But by 1534 the people of France were becoming increasingly dissatisfied with the Catholic Church. Many were followers of John Calvin, a French exile in Geneva. The French Protestants who followed Calvin became known as Huguenots. Henry II was no more lenient than his father, Francis I, but Protestantism continued to spread. Indeed it was Catherine de Medici, after her husband's death, who decided that it was simply not practical to have a policy of religious repression. The uncles of Mary Stuart, however, the de Guises, were violently opposed to Catherine's policies of conciliation. As le Balafré, Francis, duc de Guise, passed through Vassy with his partisans in March 1562, trouble erupted that resulted in the massacre of a Huguenot congregation. Thus the first civil war, a religious war, broke out in France.

Mary's father, James V, was Catholic and the son of Margaret Tudor, the sister of Henry VIII. Both James V and his wife, Mary de Guise, were Catholics and had not embraced the Church of England. However, both Mary de Guise as Queen Regent and Mary Stuart, during the brief time she actually reigned, did practice religious tolerance and tried to come to some sort of settlement or agreement with John Knox and his followers. One might imagine that despite her profound devotion to Catholicism and despite her lack of political skills, and her own impulsiveness, Mary, Queen of Scots, like Elizabeth, had no interest in looking "into the windows of men's souls." Mary Stuart was pious but not intolerant. She had beliefs but she was not dogmatic. She was not cunning nor was she slavishly in the thrall of her advisers. But she was never given the time or the opportunity to truly explore her capacities and talents as a monarch. Her instincts were good but she was often a creature of impulse. This was her worst fault.

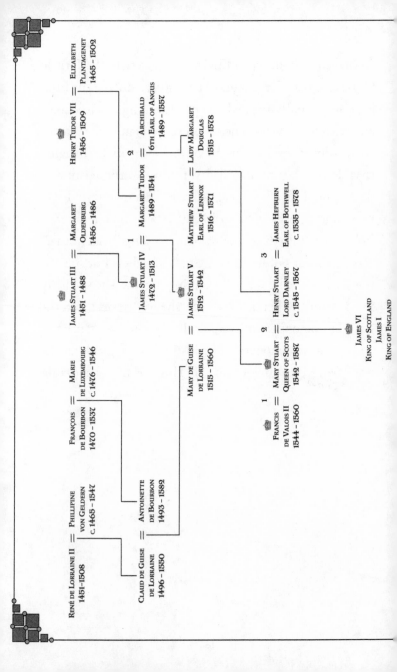

THE STUART – DE GUISE FAMILY TREE

Mary Stuart was a product of the joining of two of the most powerful ruling families of France and Scotland, the de Guises and the Stuarts. She was only a week old when she was named Queen of Scotland after the death of her father, King James V. At age 16, she was married to the Dauphin of France, 15-year-old Francis II. She also held the title of Queen of France when Francis assumed the throne after the death of his father, King Henry II. A widow at age 18, Mary later married her first cousin Henry Stuart, Lord Darnley. Together they had a son, James VI, who at 13 months old was named King of Scotland when Mary was forced to abdicate the throne. As King James I, James VI would later begin the reign of the British House of Stuarts. The chart illustrates the blending of the Stuart–de Guise families. The crown symbol indicates those who ruled. Double lines represent marriages; single lines indicate parentage. Dates of births and deaths (when available) are noted.

MARY STUART: Queen of Scotland and once Queen of France, she sought to dethrone Elizabeth I and become Queen of England. Instead, she was imprisoned for treason and beheaded on February 8, 1587.

MARY STUART'S PARENTS

JAMES STUART V: King of Scotland and the father of Mary, Queen of Scots, he was the son of King James Stuart IV and Margaret Tudor (the eldest sister of King Henry VIII of England and grandmother to Mary, Queen of Scots). James V died six days after Mary's birth in 1542, disappointed to the end that Mary had not been born the male heir he desired.

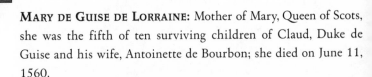

MARY DE GUISE DE LORRAINE: Mother of Mary, Queen of Scots, she was the fifth of ten surviving children of Claud, Duke de Guise and his wife, Antoinette de Bourbon; she died on June 11, 1560.

MARY STUART'S HUSBANDS

FRANCIS DE VALOIS II: Son of King Henry II and Queen Catherine de Medici of France, Francis and Mary were married on April 24, 1558. Two years later, on December 5, 1560, he died after suffering from an ear infection.

HENRY STUART, LORD DARNLEY: First cousin and second husband of Mary, Queen of Scots, he was also the grandson of Margaret Tudor; Margaret's daughter, Lady Margaret Douglas, was his mother. Darnley and Mary were married on July 29, 1565, and had one child together, James VI. Darnley died mysteriously in an explosion on February 10, 1567.

JAMES HEPBURN, EARL OF BOTHWELL: A noble from Scotland, he was Mary's third husband and suspected murderer of her second husband, Lord Darnley. He was imprisoned in Denmark where he died insane in 1578.

MARY STUART'S HEIR

JAMES STUART: Son of Mary, Queen of Scots and Henry Stuart, Lord Darnley, James VI was named King of Scotland from infancy and would also be the first of the Stuart royal family to rule England.

Portrait of Mary, Queen of Scots, Dauphine of France, at about age 18, as a young widow. By François Clouet, circa 1560.

Henry II, King of France (1547 to 1559). Undated drawing by François Clouet.

Catherine de Medici, Queen of France, wife of Henry II. Undated portrait by François Clouet.

Portrait of young Francis II, eldest son of King Henry II and Queen Catherine de Medici, and first husband of Mary Stuart.

A young Henry Stuart, Lord Darnley (circa 1555), second husband of Mary, Queen of Scots.

Nostradamus, French physician and astrologer regularly consulted by Queen Catherine de Medici. This portrait, commissioned circa 1560, is from the frontispiece to a collection of his prophecies, published in 1666.

Sixteenth-century portrait of Diane de Poitiers, mistress of Henry II and beloved mother figure to Mary Stuart.

Diane de Poitiers' castle, Château d'Anet in France, as photographed February 1975 by Marc Garanger. Designed by Philibert Delorme, the entranceway bears a cast of Benvenuto Cellini's sculpture of Diane sleeping.

Modern photograph of Château Chambord, one of Mary's and Francis II's most favorite palaces.

A view of the elegant grounds of Château Chambord, where the royal couple spent time hunting and hawking.

Modern map of Scotland and France.

An engraving of Holyrood Palace, in Edinburgh, Scotland. The palace was home to Mary, Queen of Scots and her second husband, Lord Darnley. James IV began construction of the current building around the year 1500. It was almost destroyed by fire in 1650, but was rebuilt by Charles II in the 1670s.

An older Mary, Queen of Scots, circa 1587, the year of her execution. This engraving, by artist J. Thomson, is from an original portrait in the collection of the Earl of Morton.

This painting by artist L. J. Potts depicts Mary, Queen of Scots dressed in black velvet, descending the stairs of Fotheringay Castle, Northamptonshire, England, as she is led to her execution on February 8, 1587.

The tomb of Mary, Queen of Scots in Westminster Abbey. Originally buried at Peterborough Cathedral, she was moved to this more prestigious resting place by her son, King James VI of Scotland and James I of England.

About the Author

Kathryn Lasky remembers the first time she encountered Mary, Queen of Scots: "I saw a picture of her in a book in my school library when I was in the sixth grade. There was something incredibly arresting about her appearance — tall, narrow face, tilted eyes, and from beneath her headpiece the hint of fiery red hair. She was beautiful. She was my ideal of a perfect princess."

Lasky says that when she read about historical princesses, ladies, or girls that were supposed to be beautiful, she was often disappointed when she saw their portraits, and she figured that there must have been a very different standard of beauty back then. "They all looked so severe, so forbidding. But I looked at Mary and I thought, 'I'd like to have her as a friend.' So I began to read about her."

Lasky discovered that Mary was not only beautiful, but a superb athlete as well. This made her even more appealing. Mary rode horses, played golf, hunted, and was an accomplished falconer. There were so many questions, of course, that the history books could not answer. For instance, How did it feel to be separated from your mother at four years of age? How did it feel to be betrothed before the age of five? To be raised by another family so far from your homeland? Lasky says that "to imagine the answers to these questions is what makes writing The Royal Diaries so exciting."

Kathryn Lasky is the acclaimed author of more than thirty books for children and adults. She is the author of two best-selling titles in the The Royal Diaries series, *Elizabeth I: Red Rose of the House of Tudor* and *Marie Antoinette: Princess of Versailles*. Lasky is also a prolific Dear America author, having written *A Journey to the New World: The Diary of Remember Patience Whipple; Dreams in the Golden Country: The Diary of Zipporah Feldman, a Jewish Immigrant Girl; A Time for Courage: The Diary of Kathleen Bowen;* and *Christmas After All: The Great Depression Diary of Minnie Swift*. She has also contributed *The Journal of Augustus Pelletier: The Lewis & Clark Expeditions* to the My Name is America series.

Acknowledgments

Cover painting by Tim O'Brien

Page 189: Mary, Queen of Scots, North Wind Picture Archives, Alfred, Maine.

Page 190: King Henry II, North Wind Picture Archives, Alfred, Maine.

Page 191: Catherine de Medici, North Wind Picture Archives, Alfred, Maine.

Page 192 (top): Francis II, Culver Pictures, Inc., New York, New York.

Page 192 (bottom): Lord Darnley, Hulton Getty Collection, New York, New York.

Page 193: Nostradamus, Hulton Getty Collection, New York, New York.

Page 194 (top): Diane de Poitiers, Marc Garanger/CORBIS, New York, New York.

Page 194 (bottom): Château d'Anet, Archivo Iconografico, S.A./CORBIS, New York, New York.

Page 195 (top/bottom): Château Chambord, J. Elizabeth Mills.

Page 196 (top): Map of Scotland and France, Jim McMahon.

Page 196 (bottom): Holyrood Palace, North Wind Picture Archives, Alfred, Maine.

Page 197: Mary, Queen of Scots, Culver Pictures, Inc., New York, New York.

Page 198 (top): Queen Mary being led to execution, Culver Pictures, Inc., New York, New York.

Page 198 (bottom): Mary's tomb, CORBIS, New York, New York.

OTHER BOOKS IN THE ROYAL DIARIES SERIES

ELIZABETH I
Red Rose of the House of Tudor
by Kathryn Lasky

CLEOPATRA VII
Daughter of the Nile
by Kristiana Gregory

ISABEL
Jewel of Castilla
by Carolyn Meyer

MARIE ANTOINETTE
Princess of Versailles
by Kathryn Lasky

ANASTASIA
The Last Grand Duchess
by Carolyn Meyer

NZINGHA
Warrior Queen of Matamba
by Patricia C. McKissack

KA'IULANI
The People's Princess
by Ellen Emerson White

LADY OF CHI'AO KUO
Warrior of the South
by Laurence Yep

VICTORIA
May Blossom of Britannia
by Anna Kirwan

SŎNDŎK
Princess of the Moon and Stars
by Sheri Holman

Copyright © 2002 by Kathryn Lasky.

All rights reserved. Published by Scholastic Inc., Publishers since 1920,
555 Broadway, New York, NY 10012.
SCHOLASTIC, THE ROYAL DIARIES and associated logos are trademarks
and/or registered trademarks of Scholastic Inc.

Library of Congress Cataloging-in-Publication Data
Lasky, Kathryn.
Mary, Queen of Scots, queen without a country / by Kathryn Lasky.
p. cm. — (The Royal diaries)
Includes bibliographical references
Summary: Mary, the young Scottish queen, is sent a diary from her mother in
which she records her experiences living at the court of France's King Henry II
as she awaits her marriage to Henry's son, Francis.
ISBN 0-439-19404-0
1. Mary, Queen of Scots, 1542–1587 — Childhood and youth — Juvenile
fiction. [1. Mary, Queen of Scots, 1542–1587 — Childhood and youth —
Fiction. 2. France — History — Henry II, 1547–1559 — Fiction.
3. Kings, queens, rulers, etc. — Fiction. 4. Diaries — Fiction.] I. Title.
II. Series.
PZ7.L3274 Mat 2002
[Fic] — dc21   2001031085

12 11 10 9 8 7 6 5 4   03 04 05 06

The text type was set in Augereau.
The display type was set in Aquitaine Initials.
Book design by Elizabeth B. Parisi

Printed in the U.S.A. 23
First printing, April 2002